ENTITLED TO KILL

ST. MARIN'S COZY MYSTERY 2

ACF BOOKENS

For Philip, my Daniel, the one who always takes my side and never insults my mom.

1

*I*f asked to name my favorite season, I'd immediately say fall. But I also have a deep affection for the first really warm days of spring, the ones when all the flowers are bursting forth, when tulips bejewel front yards and the cherry trees begin to flower the air with their petals.

It was late April in St. Marin's, and spring was fully here. My bookstore had been open an entire month, and it was actually turning a profit. A small profit, but a profit nonetheless. I'd even begun paying part of the mortgage on our house. Mart, my best friend and roommate, had tried to convince me to wait until at least July before I began to contribute, but I had insisted. I wasn't paying anywhere near half, but writing that first check had felt gratifying, like I'd begun to make it as a business owner.

My bookstore, All Booked Up, had been my dream for as long as I could remember. Even as a child, I'd imagined myself surrounded by books, a dog at my feet, reading all day. The business end of things came later, but mostly, I was living the dream, as they say. Okay, I didn't do as much reading as I might like, but I did have the "dog at my feet and surrounded by books" part down.

Mayhem, my trusty Black Mouth Cur sidekick, had settled right in as the shop pup, and she enjoyed welcoming the neighborhood canines – and brave felines – over for a visit, too. I had almost as many dog beds as I did armchairs in the shop, and some days, every comfy seat – both elevated and floor-level – was occupied with someone enjoying a read or a nap. And it wasn't always the dogs that were napping.

I loved that people had already begun to feel comfortable enough in the store to just come, pick up a book, and read an hour away. I didn't want to own the kind of store where people felt like they had to come in, get their books, and leave. When someone returned time and again to read the same book, I found that endearing. Not all of us have the funds to buy books, and while I was a huge patron of the local library, I fully appreciated that sometimes the best place to read was where noise was allowed and the air smelled like coffee.

Our bookstore's little café filled up what had once been the garage bay when this was a gas station. It was small and quaint, and it served the best latte this side of Annapolis. Rocky was the manager of that part of the store, and her share of the profits was helping fund her BA down at Salisbury University. Sometimes her mom, Phoebe, came in and helped out for big events, and that woman made cinnamon rolls so good they felt like a Hallmark movie Christmas morning.

I was counting on the draw of her rolls on this Saturday morning because we were having our first author event that night, and I needed to get a buzz going in town. I'd done all the usual marketing – on- and off-line – but my guest author was local, and I knew we needed the small-town crowd to make this event successful.

David Healey wrote military thrillers and mysteries set here on the Eastern Shore of Maryland, and he had a loyal readership. I just didn't know how many of those readers lived close enough by to come to the shop for his evening reading, but I was hoping that the fact that he was from Chesapeake City might bring out a banner crowd.

We'd marketed David's reading as part of a "Welcome to Spring" weekend with the hopes that people would spend at least the day, maybe even Saturday and Sunday, in St. Marin's. The hardware store had gotten in a new supply of kitschy, crab-themed T-shirts, and the art co-op had arranged a special exhibition of local artists. I had coordinated the event with the maritime museum's annual boat-skills exhibition, and Elle Heron had created a special – "Get Your Garden In Right" workshop for the afternoon. We even had a special "Eastern Shore Prix Fixe" menu set up at Chez Cuisine, a few doors down. People could come and enjoy the events of the day. The cinnamon rolls would just get the day started right.

Even if the guests didn't flock to our doors in droves, I knew I really needed a big warm concoction of flour, yeast, cinnamon, and cream cheese icing. That and Rocky's biggest latte should get me past my nerves. A lot of people were counting on this day to bolster their sales until the full-on tourist season of summer began in our waterside town, and I could feel the weight of their expectations as I unlocked the front door.

The bell that had hung over the front door of the shop since it was a gas station tinkled as I opened it, and I smiled. I would never tire of that sound.

I was swinging the door shut behind me when I felt it thud against something. I turned back to see a Basset Hound head wedged between the door and the frame. "Oh, Taco. I'm so sorry." I swung the door open. "I didn't see you there."

The Basset charged right ahead, my insulting behavior forgotten, as he saw Mayhem just ahead of me on her leash. I did my best jump rope maneuvers over the quickly tangling leashes and looked up to see Taco's owner, Daniel, smiling at me.

I felt a warm flush go up my neck and wondered if I'd ever see this man I'd been dating and not have my face turn red. We'd been a couple – that's what Mart said people in town were calling us – ever since the shop opened, but I still got all nervous when I first saw his dark hair, fair skin, and brown eyes. I found him so handsome, and he was everything my ex-husband hadn't been – reliable, attentive, and willing to take care of me even though he knew I didn't need him to do that.

Still, I was forty-four years old and totally unclear on what to call him. Was he my boyfriend? Did middle-aged women have boyfriends? *Lover* just sounded way too racy for our perfectly slow relationship, and *partner* was far too much. *Friend* didn't work either because that sounded like what my grandmother would have said, "Daniel is Harvey's 'special friend.'" I defaulted to "Daniel" instead. That worked most of the time, although a couple of times I had slipped and said, "My Daniel" as if he was a stuffed animal or I was differentiating him from another Daniel, like that guy in the lion's den I'd learned about in childhood Sunday School classes.

I liked the guy, though. A lot, even if I didn't know what to call him. And Mayhem felt much the same about his pup, Taco. I didn't really buy into the whole dog love affairs craze myself, but these two were at the least best pals.

Already, they'd sniffed out the best bed for the day – the one in the front window's sunbeam beside the display of books on shipwrecks – and were lying butt to butt and snoring. The dog's life was something.

As Daniel and I made our way to the front counter, he gave me a quick kiss on the cheek. "So aside from trying to decapitate my dog, how has your day been so far?"

"Well, I have to say it just got a whole lot better." I had never been a flirtatious person before, but this man, for some reason he brought it out in me.

A blush flew into his cheeks, too, and we stood grinning at one another until the sound of a throat clearing broke our gaze. Rocky was standing in front of the counter across from us with a grin a mile wide on her face. "Sorry. I thought you'd heard me come in."

I looked toward the front door. I *hadn't* heard the bell ring. "No, I'm sorry. How are you? How's studying for finals going?"

She let out a long, slow sigh. "It's going." She pulled her thick handful of tiny braids into a hair tie and then dropped a heavy tote bag onto the counter. "I mean, I love my classes, but I had a very high opinion of my reading speed and retention ability when I signed up for three English and two history classes. Finals are in two weeks, and I have five books to read and three papers to write to even get to the finals."

"Whew, that's a lot. What are your professors thinking?" I remembered my college days when I was an English and History double major just like Rocky. One semester, I'd had to buy sixty-seven books. Sixty-seven. I loved books, but that was ridiculous.

"They're thinking that their class is the most important one. They've all forgotten what it's like to have five classes and a job."

Daniel laughed. "That, right there, ladies, is why I didn't finish college. Too much reading."

I never in my life thought I'd date a man who didn't read, but here I was, full on in the throes of like – I wasn't ready for the other L word yet – with a man who took it as a point of pride that the last full book he read was the copy of *Tom and Jerry Meet Little Quack* that his mom found in a box of his first-grade mementos.

It wasn't that Daniel didn't appreciate knowledge or books, and it certainly wasn't that he wasn't smart – the man could disassemble and then reassemble a car engine in less than two hours, a feat I understood to be impressive, even though my knowledge of cars stopped at the fact that Brits called the trunk of the car the "boot." No, Daniel was plenty smart. He just couldn't sit still long enough to read. His body needed to be moving. Even when we watched TV – lately, we'd been binge-watching a show I'd loved a few years back, *The 4400* – he put together model cars. He just couldn't be completely still, and school required a lot of stillness.

I didn't mind the car-building stuff, though, because he'd inspired me to make use of my downtime, too. I'd picked back up my cross-stitch hobby after years of neglect. And like most things in my life, I didn't start slow. I bought a kit of a cat in a bookshop. It was beautiful – all bright colors and a black and white cat with a few extra pounds that reminded me of my own girl, Aslan. But it was also immense – maybe 18 x 24 on small-count fabric – and every square called for a stitch. At this rate, I'd finish it in when I was seventy. Still, it was relaxing because it required my attention and let my mind slow down. It was the only way I'd found, so far, to stop thinking about the shop. Well, cross-stitch and kissing Daniel.

Rocky hefted her heavy bag onto her shoulder and headed to the café while Daniel carried the platter of her mom's cinnamon rolls behind her. I'd slipped one out from under the plastic and sat savoring the doughy goodness while I checked emails.

Everything seemed to be in order for the day. David Healey had written to say he'd be in town by noon and wondered if I could grab lunch to talk about the night's event. I shot back a quick response with my cell number and told him to text me when he arrived. Then, I answered enough queries about parking and general activities in town that by the time we opened at ten, I felt confident we were going to have a great day.

ABOUT TEN THIRTY, Mart arrived with Cate, our friend who ran the art coop. They'd been out on the bay kayaking, trying to capture photos of some watermen at work for Cate's new portrait series. Mart was on hand to run the register in case things got busy, and Cate was going to lead a plein air painting group that was meeting here at eleven. Both of them were rosy cheeked and equally pleasant tempered. Part of me wished I'd been able to go, but most of me was quite content to have spent the morning answering questions about books, making notes about titles we needed to order back in, and enjoying Phoebe's cinnamon roll. Sure, I missed out on some things by running the shop, but what I got to do, well, it more than made up for it.

"Looks like you've got things well in hand," Mart said.

"Now, let's not be too hasty, Martha." Cate put on a serious face as she brushed her short black hair out of her eyes. "The true test is whether she—"

I reached below the counter and pulled out two saucers, each adorned with a cinnamon roll.

Cate laughed. "Yep, all in hand here."

When I'd met Cate a few weeks ago, I hadn't realized that Mart and I really needed a third to make our friendship even more amazing, but it turns out that the third we were missing was a short, Korean-American photographer whose husband cooked really, really well.

Mart and I had been friends for years back in San Francisco, and when I'd decided to return home to Maryland last fall, she'd decided to come along. She, by far, looked the youngest of all of us with her fair skin that showed nary a wrinkle and her thick, brown hair that she wore in soft waves or in a ponytail that, somehow, managed to look amazing. My curly, quickly-graying short hair did not always fare so well in the wind and moisture of a waterside town, and I took to rolled bandanas on days when I didn't want to look like Lyle Lovett or to spend an hour with a flat iron. (I never wanted to spend an hour with a flat-iron.) Also, I had wrinkles in my pale, pinkish skin, including a furrow between my eyes that would never smooth out again.

Many women never get to have one good friend in the world, and I was lucky enough to have two. In both literal and figurative ways, they had each saved my life, and I was so glad we got to see each other every day, even if they teased me no end about having a boyfriend. They always insisted on saying it *boooyyyfriend*, like we were eleven. Still, I adored them.

My friends tucked into their cinnamon rolls with all the genteelness of vultures on roadkill, and I couldn't help but smile. No pinkies in the air here. I'm pretty sure I even caught Mart licking the plate when I turned around to get more bags to put under the counter.

Snacks done and coffee procured from Rocky, they got to work, and I began my usual circuit around the store, just to be sure things were tidy, but not pristine. Something about a little bit of disheveled order felt home-like, comfortable.

I was just rounding the corner of the religion section when I spied a familiar pair of Jordans propped on a shelf next to a wing-back chair. I slipped behind the seat and peeked over the top to get a look at the title of the book the person was reading. "*The Water Dancer*. I hear that's really good."

Marcus Dawson slowly lowered his book, pulled his brown legs down as I stepped around in front of him, and smiled up at me. "It's amazing," he said, "but no spoilers. You have to read it yourself."

"Will do." I kicked his shin playfully. "You know, you don't have to be here when you're not working."

He shrugs. "What can I say? When you find a good thing . . ."

Marcus had started working here almost a month ago, and he was amazing at his job – thoughtful with his recommendations and voracious in his reading. At first, I'd hired him to help him out, but it turned out that he was a major draw for returning customers who found his book suggestions to be so fitting for them that they came in just to talk to him about the previous recommendation and pick up a new one.

Now, he had a regular column in our weekly newsletter, where he did book matchmaking with customers who filled out a short survey as they stopped by. I'd gotten the idea from one of my favorite podcasts, *What Should I Read Next?*, and people were loving it. Our box of completed surveys was so full that we were talking about doing Instagram videos to accommodate more customer requests. I had definitely gotten the better end of the deal when I'd hired Marcus.

On Monday, he would begin his first shift as assistant manager. I noticed he'd had his hair cut into a shorter version of his typical box fade and wondered again if all the things from my teenage years were coming back: high-waisted jeans, fanny packs, and shoulder pads. It made me shiver. Marcus's hair though, I loved. I couldn't help but think of Kid 'n Play when I saw him, but I wouldn't make the mistake of mentioning them again since Marcus had looked at me like I was approximately eight hundred years old the one time I'd brought them up.

I'd given him the weekend off so that he could relax, spend time with his mom, and maybe even do something fun in Annapolis or Baltimore, but I wasn't all that surprised to see him in the store. He really did seem to love St. Marin's and my bookshop, and I knew that living in his apartment above Daniel's garage

was probably kind of lonely, especially when Daniel wasn't at
work. Plus, I just liked him and liked having him around.

"Well, happy reading. But no working today. Not even Insta
photos. It's your day off. I don't want to pay you, but I'll be
forced to if you work, you hear me?" I gave his leg another
nudge and headed off to help Daniel, who was bringing up two
boxes of books for the new window display.

Max Davies, the owner of Chez Cuisine, had taken a while to
grow on me, but it turned out that he had great taste in cookbooks. I'd promised him we'd do a new display with some titles
he'd recommended. It had taken a bit of coaxing for me to
convince him that we needed not only true cookbooks but also
some other titles – like Ruth Reichl's *Save Me The Plums* – to
round out the display. But his list of recommendations turned
out to be stellar and diverse, and I was eager to get the books
into the window for the afternoon.

Daniel hefted the boxes onto the display platform and gave me a
quick hug before heading over to his garage. For the past couple
of weeks, he'd spent the first couple of hours of Saturday
morning here at the shop helping me with displays and shelv-
ing. He wasn't much of a reader, but he was *all in* for supporting
the shop. Today, though, he had car repairs to manage, so I
focused on my display and looked forward to seeing him later.

I had just put the final book – *Eat This Poem* by Nicole Gulotta –
into the display when David pulled up. Mart and I helped him
unload his car, and then he and I headed out for lunch at the
new BBQ place that had just opened up at the end of Main
Street. I was a sucker for a place with a cute name, so Piggle and
Shake had won me over as soon as the sign went up.

The author and I had a lovely lunch, and I was thrilled to hear
that he had more books coming in his renovation series. I knew

his military thrillers were good, too, but I was much more a mystery girl myself.

After our meal, I pointed him in the direction of the co-op and gave him the address for the maritime museum before heading back to the shop for the afternoon. St. Marin's wasn't San Francisco in terms of entertainment, but in some ways, it was even better. At least here, everything was within easy walking distance of everything else. Plus, since I knew Cate would take good care of David at the co-op and then Lucas would do the same at the museum, I didn't worry that he might get bored or frustrated. They'd agreed to give him the behind-the-scenes tour and have him back to the shop by five so we could all get dinner before the reading.

On my way back, I needed to stop by Elle Heron's farm stand to pick up some fresh flowers for the café tables and a bouquet for the signing table, too. Elle, a white woman in her sixties with light-brown hair cut into a bob, had been supplying fresh flowers – all grown at her small farm outside of town – since we opened, and this time, she was giving us some of the most amazing tulips I'd ever seen. The bright reds and yellows and purples would add just the right color to the store, and I couldn't wait to see what she'd put together for the main arrangement.

I shed my sweater as I walked the two blocks up to her shop – No Label; Just Farm to Table – and took a swig from my water bottle before I walked in. The day had grown quite warm, and I had broken my first sweat of the year, which was cause for a small celebration that I'd begun a decade ago in my first "summer" on the west side of San Francisco. There, the warm days come in mid-fall, when the fog burns off completely and the temperature climbs into the high seventies, maybe even low eighties. On each of those days, I walked to the corner market and got an ice cream from the chest freezer by the front door.

Always the same thing every day until the fog returned. Sadly, "summer" in San Francisco rarely lasted more than two weeks.

Now, I was going to keep up that tradition with a slight modification. After all, I couldn't each ice cream every day it got to eighty here. I wouldn't have minded eating ice cream every day from April to September, but I figured my cholesterol might mind. So just the first day, I decided. A celebration of the warmth returning.

"Hey Elle." I shouted as I walked toward the cooler, hopeful that she was as down-to-earth in her ice cream selection as she was about everything else. I wanted my plain, classic ice cream sandwich something fierce, and I was not disappointed.

I slid open the top of the freezer, and as I leaned down and grabbed my sandwich, something caught my eye. I stood up and took a step back.

Then, I dropped my ice cream on the floor as I backed into a shelf of broccoli and cabbage seedlings and sent potting soil and tiny plants flying.

Beside the cooler lay the body of Huckabee Harris, his muck boots covered in mud and his face as white as the vanilla ice cream now leaking out of the wrapper at my feet.

2

*E*lle had come out from the backroom just as her plant display toppled over. She'd followed my line of vision and let out a commendable squeak when she saw Harris on the floor.

As I took out my phone and called 911, she waved me behind the counter and away from the body. Unfortunately, we'd had a shared experience with crime scenes before, so we knew not to touch anything, even though everything in me wanted to drape a sheet or something over Huckabee Harris's pale, white face.

Harris wasn't my favorite person. I don't think most people liked him, in fact. He was loud and crude, and he insisted on talking on his flip phone wherever he was, no matter what was going on around him. Two weeks ago, I'd had to ask him to step outside to discuss his bunions instead of carrying on the discussion about Epsom salts and foot massages in the café at the shop. He'd stood up, stepped right into my face, and begun detailing his foot-sanding regimen until I gave up and walked away.

Still, no one deserved to die the way he had. He looked terrified, like something had snuck up on him and scared him to death.

Sheriff Mason arrived at the store within minutes, took one look at the scene, and asked me to step outside. I knew he needed to separate Elle and me to take our statements, so I moved quickly and waited on the bench outside Elle's shop.

A few minutes later, the sheriff sat down beside me, let me tell him what happened, and then closed his notebook. "Okay, well, that's pretty straightforward. Any theories?"

I looked sharply at him. "You're asking my opinion about a murder. Is this some sort of reverse psychology to keep me from butting in again?" The sheriff had been very patient with my sleuthing in the past, but I knew he wasn't keen to have my input.

"Not exactly reverse psychology. Just hoping that asking directly might get any desire to investigate out of your system."

I smiled. "Nope, no theories here. Most people didn't like him, though."

"That's putting it mildly. Last week, he stormed into our office and demanded I arrest his neighbors because," the sheriff rubbed his forehead so hard I thought he might bruise himself, "they were building a house in a place – on their property, mind you – that would limit the directions he could shoot deer from his own front porch come hunting season."

I gave the sheriff a puzzled look. "Is that legal, I mean to hunt from your front porch?"

"It is, but I don't love it. Too easy to shoot recklessly. Plus, the deer never have a chance. But technically, yes, it's legal." He sighed. "What is not legal is to shoot toward another person's home. Harris knew that, so he thought that people shouldn't be able to build in his 'hunting zone,' as he called it."

I didn't think I had an eye roll big enough for that idea, but I restrained myself out of respect for the dead.

The sheriff shook his head. "Anyway, there will be no shortage of people who didn't like Harris, I'm afraid. Can't figure any of them would want to kill the man, though."

"Sigh. Do we know how he died?"

He looked at me out of the corner of his eye. "*We* don't know anything yet, Harvey." Then, *he* sighed, "The cause of death will take some time."

"DNA?"

Another sideways glance. "You watch too much police TV, Harvey. Maybe switch to reality shows. I hear Daniel really likes that gold mining one." He turned to face me then. "But yes, we will check for DNA. You do know, though, that the TV shows get this one right. You have to have DNA to match it against. How many of St. Marin's residents do you think are in CODIS, Harvey?"

I felt my heartrate kick up with excitement. "How many?"

It was the sheriff's turn to roll his eyes. "It was a rhetorical question, Harvey. I have no idea, but I can tell you, not many."

Sheriff Tucker Mason was a St. Marin's native. He'd grown up here, gone away to college at University of Maryland, and then come back to the Eastern Shore to go to the police academy before serving as a deputy for fifteen years and then successfully running for election to the position as sheriff, the first African American sheriff in the county's history. He had a reputation as quite the prankster, and I'd felt like I'd been completely accepted in town when he asked the cross-country team from the high school to stop by on their afternoon training run on Tuesday because they thought Mayhem might need a little more exercise. At first I'd been puzzled, but then I saw that they had a huge flag that said, "Support Harvey Beckett's bookshop so she can walk her own dog." I knew their route wound all through St.

Marin's and then out the major routes into town before heading into the small farm roads, which meant *everyone* was going to see the sign. I wanted to be miffed, but I couldn't help but laugh.

The sheriff had stopped by just about the time the team had brought back an exhausted Mayhem, and he'd almost doubled over in laughter when he saw my face.

"I should have known I had you to thank for this bit of publicity," I said with mock anger.

He dropped an arm around my shoulder. "Glad you've joined us, Harvey." He gave me a little squeeze and then climbed back into his patrol car, still laughing.

The next day, business did tick up a bit, and I only had to fend off two over-the-top animal lovers who were worried about Mayhem's welfare. When they saw her sound asleep on a dog bed that looked like a leather sofa, complete with tufting and a chenille throw (a gift from a customer who LOVED bringing in her miniature pinscher and wanted her to have a comfy bed), they quickly retreated to the animal section and invested in copies of *Marley and Me* and *The Art of Racing in the Rain.*

Needless to say, our sheriff wasn't the stuff of stereotypes. I really liked him because he didn't take himself too seriously even as he was very good at his job.

He wasn't joking today, though. Today, he had a murderer to find. After he got our statements, he asked us to leave the shop to him for a bit while his tech team and the coroner finished up, so Elle walked back to my store with me.

"I didn't hear a thing," she said as we reached the first cross street and waited for the car at the corner to turn. "Not a thing. I didn't even know he was in the store. I was so focused on finishing up the arrangements for tonight's reading that I wasn't paying that much attention. I assume people will ring the bell when they're ready to check out." She looked a little peaked, so I slipped my arm through hers.

"I totally understand." I gave her arm a squeeze. "I'm glad you didn't hear anything. If someone wants to do something like that," I suppressed a shudder, "I don't know that you could have stopped them. And if you'd tried . . ."

Even more color drained from her face. "I know CPR. Maybe I could have saved him."

I stopped walking and held her beside me before turning her to face me. "This isn't your fault, okay? It's really unfortunate that Harris died, and particularly unfortunate for you that he died in your shop. But you did nothing wrong, and I don't think you could have done anything to save him, okay?"

She let out a hard breath. "Okay." I saw her set her shoulders as she turned back up the sidewalk toward my store. "Still, I wish I could have done something."

I nodded. I felt the same way. Three times now I'd found people's bodies, and three times I felt helpless, but guilty, too, like I should have been able to help. Even though in every case the person had been very dead. Maybe feeling guilty was better than feeling helpless? I didn't know.

When we reached the bookstore, I sent Elle right over to Rocky for a cup of chamomile tea and a piece of shortbread and told Mart the whole story.

"Huckabee Harris. The farmer? That guy who complained that we had too many books by women in the window? Is it unkind to say good riddance?"

"Martha Weston!" I whispered.

"Okay, sorry. I don't mean that, of course, but gracious, that dude was a pain in the rear." One of the things I loved most about Mart was that she always said what she thought. Okay, I almost always loved that trait. Now, I was just glad that the sheriff wasn't here to overhear her musings. He would know that Mart had not done this, of course, but no need to cloud the water of suspects.

"Yeah, the sheriff is down there now. Fortunately, he's keeping things discrete so that it doesn't disrupt the activities today. Well, except for at Elle's shop. Poor thing. She feels horrible because she didn't know he was even in there." I looked over at our friend and was glad to see Rocky tending to her so well.

"Well, that's a first. Huckabee Harris seemed to make his presence known wherever he went. Wonder why he was so quiet in Elle's shop."

"Good question." I could feel the cogs starting to turn in my brain, but I didn't have enough to go on . . . yet. "I expect we'll know more soon." I glanced down at the clock on the register screen. "Oh my word. Is it already four? Crap. I've got to get the store set up."

"Right. I'll start organizing the chairs for the reading." Mart was already headed toward the storeroom to pull out the brand-new folding chairs I'd picked up from the warehouse store last week. "You were thinking we'd set up in the fiction section, right?" she called over her shoulder.

"Yep. Maybe fifteen chairs to start?" I'd thought about having the reading in the café but had decided being surrounded by books was more fitting. We could always spread out into the aisle by history if we needed to. But if the crowd was small, planning for an intimate event seemed smarter. No need to embarrass David Healey or make people uncomfortable if only a few folks showed.

Man, I hoped more than a few folks showed up.

. . .

AT FIVE THIRTY, David came back to the shop, and he and I walked over to Chez Cuisine to meet Daniel, Cate, Lucas, and Elle. Her store had been cleared about an hour before, so she'd rushed back and forth between her shop and mine to get the flowers and place them all. I figured she needed a good meal, so I invited her along, hoping against hope that Max Davies wouldn't throw a conniption about the need for one extra chair.

I was thrilled to see his restaurant was quite full because I liked when my fellow business owners thrived and because I was hoping a lot of these folks were coming over to the store for the reading. I was even happier when his hostess easily pulled one extra chair up for Elle at our reserved round table in the back corner of the restaurant. Our meal was delicious, even for me, the woman who lived in a waterside town but hated seafood. Appetizers were oysters on the half-shell and these stuffed mushrooms that I wanted to shove in all my pockets. Then, we had Max's signature coq au vin and risotto, followed by the best crème brulee I'd ever eaten. I felt just like Amelie in the movie when I smacked my spoon against the top and heard the crack. Oddly, Max came out and asked me – and only me – how I had liked the meal. When I told him it was delicious and everyone echoed my words, he bowed, took my hand, and kissed it. I shot Cate a puzzled look that she gave right back to me, and I felt Daniel's gaze but didn't know what to say, so just avoided looking at him until Max left and we resumed our conversation.

By the time we got up to leave, we were all roly-poly with good food and very relaxed from three great bottles of wine. Even if the reading only brought a small crowd, I already considered the night a success, and I thought David felt the same way from the small smile on his face.

But things only got better. When we arrived back at the shop, I saw that Mart and Rocky had pulled out every chair we had, including all the café seats and every moveable arm chair, because the store was packed. A quick headcount brought me to sixty people, and a few guests were still coming in for the seven p.m. reading.

David gave me a big grin as I handed him two bottles of water and he propped himself on the stool at the front of the crowd and let me give my welcome and introduction. The reading went fabulously, and we sold all the copies of his books that we had on hand and even placed a few special orders for more.

By the time the last customer left, it was after nine, and I was worn out, but thrilled. I couldn't believe our first author event had gone so well, and David thanked me profusely as he left to make the drive north to go home.

My friends stayed to help us put the store back in order, and then we all dropped into chairs in the café for a few minutes to debrief and enjoy some hot tea. "Well, that certainly brought the day to an end on a better note," Elle said as she sipped her peppermint brew.

"I'll say." I was so glad the event had gone well, but I was also happy to see that Elle seemed to be feeling better. But then, I noticed the confused glance that passed between Cate and Lucas. "Oh gracious. You hadn't heard? I found Huckabee Harris dead in Elle's shop early this afternoon."

I watched Cate's face go from surprise to what looked like delight to a carefully composed serious glower. "Wow. Yeah, we hadn't heard." Her voice was a few notes lower than usual as she attempted to sound sorrowful. It didn't work.

Lucas shook his head next to her. "I'm sorry to hear that. Really. But I can't say that I'll miss him much."

"That seems to be the consensus," Mart said.

"I couldn't stand that man, but still, no one deserves to die." Cate's voice was back to its normal pitch, and she hugged her shoulders. A gentle quiet settled over the room, fatigue and the sadness of death catching up to us.

I was just about to stand and begin the exodus for the evening when a loud banging on the glass above my head startled me. It was Marcus, and he looked terrified.

I rushed over, unlocked the door, and barely got it open before Marcus barreled in. "Harvey, I need your help. The sheriff just called me. He's on his way to my apartment." His voice was squeaky, and he was breathless.

I put my hand on his arm. "Okay, Marcus. Why is the sheriff coming to your apartment?" I figured there must be something the sheriff needed, maybe some help with the 5K that was going on in town tomorrow or something.

"He's coming to arrest me. He says that an eyewitness saw me kill Huckabee Harris." His eyes were wide, and I thought he might cry. "Harvey, I don't even know who Huckabee Harris is."

Rocky put on a fresh pot of decaf. I had called the sheriff and let him know that Marcus was at the shop with us and that he could meet him there. I figured as long as Marcus wasn't hiding it didn't matter where the sheriff came to get him. Plus, I had a small hope that we might be able to avoid an arrest altogether if we could work through some things.

As we waited for the sheriff and Rocky set an emergency supply of shortbread on the table by Marcus, I asked him to explain what the sheriff had said. He took a deep breath and said, "He said that someone had reported seeing me at your shop," he looked at Elle, "early this afternoon, about the time this man Huckabee Harris was killed. But I wasn't there. I was here all afternoon."

"I'll tell the sheriff I saw you here, Marcus, reading."

"And I'll let him know that you were working," Mart said with a quick glance at me. "I tried to stop him, Harvey, but the man can't help himself. He kept recommending books left and right. He only left the shop a few minutes before you came back in."

"See, I couldn't have killed that man." Marcus's voice was still quite shaky.

Cate leaned over and put her hand over Marcus's. "Marcus, I assure you that no one here thinks you killed anyone." We all nodded, and the tension in Marcus's face eased a little.

Just then, there was a knock on the front door, and I walked over to let the sheriff in. "Sheriff, thanks for coming here. He was so scared."

"I know. I hated to call him like that, but I thought it might be better for me to just come by his apartment casually rather than make a public arrest." He gestured out the window with his chin. "Even drove my personal car to keep things quiet."

I smiled at my friend. "That was kind of you. But between you and me, you don't think Marcus actually did this do you?"

He shook his head. "No, I don't. But this witness is adamant. Insists she saw him there at the time of the murder."

I sighed. "Well, we have witnesses here, a lot of them, including me and Mart, who know he was here all afternoon. That he didn't leave until around four p.m."

"Alright then." A smile lit up the sheriff's face. "Then all I'll need are your statements, and we can keep from making any arrests tonight."

As we walked over toward the café, he said, "Is that coffee?"

"You tell Marcus the good news, and I'll pour you a cup myself."

• • •

THE NEXT MORNING, when I arrived at the shop about nine thirty, Marcus was waiting. He looked better than he had the night before, but I could tell something was still bothering him. He was pacing back and forth in front of the store with his head down and his hands deep in his pockets.

"Marcus? You okay?"

He jolted a bit when I spoke. "What? Oh yeah, I'm okay. Just wanted to talk to you about something."

"Okay. Let's go." We opened up the shop, and I gave Marcus his own set of keys so he wouldn't have to wait outside for me anymore. Then, he fell right into the routine of turning on lights, checking on the dog water bowls, and starting the coffeepots that Rocky had set up the night before. I let him work, even though it was his day off, because it seemed like it was helpful for him to move in his routine.

When the store was all set for opening, we still had fifteen minutes before I unlocked the door, so we tucked ourselves into the two wingchairs by the psychology section. "Okay, what's up?"

He looked up at the ceiling and said, "Harvey, why would someone accuse me of murder?"

I had wondered the same thing when I woke up about two a.m. I had always been one of those people who could drop off to sleep with no trouble, but if something woke me for long enough in the middle of the night, I could worry myself into a near panic attack before getting back to sleep. My cat Aslan both loved and loathed – when I petted her a minute too long – this trait. Last night, my concerns about Marcus led me to over-petting and four pinpricks of warning in the back of my hand.

"I don't know, Marcus. I kind of thought about that, too." I was understating the two hours I'd spent obsessing, but the man was already concerned enough. No need to heap my worries onto his. "I can't imagine you'd have any enemies, anyone who wanted to get you in trouble."

He shook his head. "Nope. I'm not really a 'making enemies' kind of guy."

I knew what he meant. From what I could see, Marcus was liked by everyone, even if at first some folks, including Lucas, had thought he was kind of angry at the world. He'd had reason to be angry, but I'd never thought he was. Just thought he was a kid who'd been dealt a kind of rough hand.

I folded my left leg under my right and put my hands behind my head to ponder how it would be that someone would identify Marcus as a killer. I had asked the sheriff the night before if this was a "meets the description" situation.

The sheriff had looked me dead in the eye and said, "Harvey Beckett, do you really think *I* would act on one of those reports about black people being 'out of place?'"

I hadn't, of course, but given how many people seem to report black men doing things they didn't do simply because they were, well, black, I felt like I had to ask.

"No, Harvey. The witness named Marcus specifically. Said they recognized his shoes."

"His Jordans?"

"Yes." It took a kind of special eye to know tennis shoes, and I didn't have that eye. I only knew they were Jordans because Mart told me. She had an eye for shoes, especially sneakers. They were her one luxury purchase – a new pair every month. Her closet was lined with neat shelves displaying all her pairs, grouped by brand and then color. It was a rainbow of Asics, New Balance, Converse, and Jordans. When someone made a joke about women and their shoes, Mart pulled out her camera, loaded a photo, and asked, "Like this?" Since it wasn't the stereotypical collection of heels and boots, the person almost always bit their tongue.

"It's not unusual to wear Jordans, is it?"

The sheriff had rolled his eyes. "No, Harvey. But I know you know those aren't your run-of-the-mill Jordans. The witness knew they were Air Jordan 1s, the originals."

I blew out a whistle. "So they were naming Marcus specifically, then? Not just saying they saw someone who looked like him."

"Exactly." He put on his hat. "Thanks for taking care of him, Harvey."

I smiled. "No problem. Oh, and I've already forgotten. Who did you say the witness was?"

"Goodnight, Harvey." The sheriff walked out the front door.

Now, with Marcus so bothered by this accusation, I didn't know whether to tell him that someone had specifically fingered him or try to just play it off that it might have been a case of mistaken identity. I started to say, "You know, they might have just seen a black man . . ." but even saying that in my mind told me that was a mistake. Racism was alive and well, but it didn't help end it to fabricate a profiling situation when there wasn't one. We had enough real profiling to deal with.

I sat forward and put my elbows on my knees before looking at Marcus. "The sheriff said they ID'ed your shoes, Marcus. Someone definitely wanted to point the finger at you."

He dropped his head back against the seat. "I was hoping I was overreacting."

"Yeah. But look at it this way, this is our first clue in figuring out who the actual murderer is."

He gave me a sideways glance. "Harvey, there are about three hundred things wrong with that sentence, starting with the fact that *we* aren't the ones trying to solve this murder." He raised his eyebrows. "Additionally, just because someone tried to set me up doesn't mean they were actually the murderer."

"You're right. . . about both things. But first of all, you know me." I gave him my own significant look. "Second, it doesn't mean they committed the murder, but it does seem to indicate they were trying to misdirect the sheriff's attention away from whoever did, don't you think?"

He shook his head. "Maybe. But—"

Just then, a knock at the front door drew my attention, and I saw Galen Gilbert outside with Mack, his English Bulldog. I glanced down at my watch. Ten a.m. on the dot. Time to open. "Don't worry, Marcus. We'll get this all sorted."

"Thanks, Harvey," he said as he stood up. "I decided to go over to Annapolis today, see Mom." He walked me to the door. "Unless you need me."

"I love that idea. Get out of here." I opened the front door, let Galen in, and gave Marcus a solid push out. "I'll see you tomorrow, Mr. Assistant Manager."

That brought a smile to his face. "See you tomorrow."

Galen let Mack off her leash and wandered toward the register with me. "So Marcus is your new assistant? I love that idea. That young man knows his books. Did you know he has read everything Agatha Raisin mystery? He told me he really likes how loveable she is, but that he's not sure why James puts up with her. I concurred completely." He looked over toward the mystery section. "Anyway, great choice in assistants, Harvey. I'm off to shop."

Galen had started coming into the shop shortly after we opened, picking up his weekly selection of mystery novels to read and review on his very, very popular Instagram feed. Not many men read mysteries, and even fewer admitted it when they did. But Galen had firmly embraced his love affair with the genre, and boldly shared his recommendations with tens of thousands of followers every week. He had promised to give me bookstagramming lessons soon, and I couldn't wait. I had a lot to learn about my grid and my color palette and all the things Insta that Galen said would soon become second nature.

I stifled a giggle at the absurdity of a sixty-something-year-old white guy being an Instagram influencer. Sometimes, life is better than fiction.

I glanced over to see Mayhem and Mack sniffing around the front of Rocky's bakery cabinet, and only then realized she hadn't come in yet. That wasn't like her at all, but when I pulled out my phone, I saw a text.

Car broke down. Daniel on his way. Be in as soon as possible. Can you start coffee?

I dashed off a quick reply to let her know it was all under control and then went to turn on the two coffeepots and shoo away the sniffy dogs. While I waited for the brew to finish and kept an eye on the register, I pondered why someone would kill Harris. Was there something to be gained, or was it revenge? A love triangle? I clearly had been reading too many YA novels. There was always a love triangle in those.

When the alarms on the pots sounded, I was no closer to having an answer, but I figured a good dose of caffeine might help. I filled the carafes and put out the half and half and skim, checked to be sure the sugar options were supplied, and then headed back to the shop.

Within minutes, Rocky came blustering in, an apology on her lips. "Your car broke down, Rocky. No need to apologize." I looked around at the few customers in the shop. "It's been a slow start. You're fine. Take your time settling in."

She gave me a grateful look and headed to the café, just as Daniel came in the front door. He made his way over to where I was standing near the poetry books and gave me a kiss on the cheek.

"Glad you could help Rocky out. It won't be an expensive repair, right? I know she can't afford anything big."

"Not expensive at all." He glanced at the café and then lowered his voice. "She just ran out of gas."

I looked over at Rocky, who seemed overly focused on her work. "Oh poor thing. It's never happened to me, but I'm always afraid it will."

"I believe that. I've seen how close to empty you run. Maybe take Rocky's experience as a cautionary tale."

I knew he was right, but sometimes it just wasn't convenient to stop for gas. I had podcasts to listen to, after all. Since moving to St. Marin's, my risky gas fill-up ways put me in less and less danger since I almost never drove. I lived within walking distance of the shop, and since I worked every day, I didn't even get in my old Subaru wagon very often.

Daniel started the old girl up and ran it around town for me every couple of weeks. "Cars don't do well when they just sit," he said again and again. I was happy to have him take care of something I didn't care enough about to tend. I figured I returned the favor by making sure he had more than enough cheap beer and cheese dip in his fridge.

Still, I felt terrible for Rocky. She was precise about being on time, and I knew she was mortified at her oversight. I glanced over again and saw she was filling the pastry case like normal and decided to just leave it be. Even trying to be kind would probably be humiliating at this point.

"Anyway, thanks for helping her. You're our knight in—" I never finished my sentence because just then, my parents walked in. Burt and Sharon Beckett were sticklers about manners but never had been big on courtesy. They lived less than an hour away and had only been to visit once. I'd invited them for David's reading the night before, but they'd had plans to play Settlers of Catan – "It's all the rage," my mom had said when she'd told me – and didn't want to change it for something as pesky as their daughter's first author event in her new store. They hadn't made the grand opening of the shop or the big street fair I'd organized a few weeks back either.

But here they were today without notice. I let out a long sigh. I'd long ago learned that changing them was not possible and confronting them only made me suffer, so I smiled and waved as I said, "My parents are here," to Daniel through clenched teeth. "I've told them about you," I said as I pretended to straighten the shelf behind the register, "but they will act like I have not. It's their MO. So sorry." But that was all I had time to stay before they reached us.

Dad gave me a good solid hug, but I could feel him looking around the shop over my head. And Mom only hugs with her forearms. Body contact makes her uncomfortable. She, however, was far less interested in the shop than in the man who was standing behind the register next to me.

"I'm Sharon, Harvey's mother, and you are?"

"I'm Daniel Galena, Mrs. Beckett. Harvey has told me all about you."

He was completely lying. I mean I'd told him that my parents and I weren't close, but I appreciated that he set the playing field clearly. He knew who she was, so she'd look foolish or just plain cruel if she didn't say the same.

I saw Mom wince slightly, but then, she regained her prim composure and said, "Ah yes, Daniel. Harvey has mentioned you." She glanced down at his hands. "You're a plumber or something, aren't you?"

"A mechanic, ma'am, but I'm fine with a pipe snake, too." Daniel was a pretty shy fellow, but I was thrilled to see him refusing to play my mother's game of coy derision. He shot me a quick wink. "Mr. Beckett, nice to *finally* meet you, sir."

Gracious, that man was amazing. I loved that subtle weight on *finally*. He was due a full back massage later as gratitude.

My dad turned from his scrutiny of the business section just past the register and said, "Daniel, nice to meet you. Tell me – worked on any notable vehicles lately?"

They headed off toward the café, and Daniel gave me a quick smile as if to say, "I'm fine, and I'm here." I felt myself relax just a little. But then, my mother said, "So I see business isn't as good as you'd hoped."

I glanced around. We weren't packed, but six or seven people were browsing – that was pretty good for a Sunday morning in a town where most people went to church every Sunday. "Actually, this isn't bad. We'll pick up the after-church crowd come one o'clock or so."

"I see," she said and then ran a hand over – but never through – the dark brown coif that was, miraculously, the exact same shade of brunette it had been when I was five. Her weekly hair appointment was on Thursdays at four thirty, and, growing up, we'd always had fish sticks and apple sauce on those nights.

Now, it's salmon and Pinot Grigio for her and steak and an IPA for my dad. But only after her hair appointment.

She turned a full 360 degrees to look at the store and then said, "So you still haven't been able to hire any help, I see?" She tried to make her voice sound concerned, but really, condescension was all I could hear.

"Actually, my assistant manager starts full-time tomorrow. I gave him the weekend off before he begins that position." I tried not to look smug, but I think my face gave me away.

"Well, then . . ." She gave another survey around the shop. "Is it wise to bring on someone full-time? I mean."

I laughed, and my mother finally met my gaze. "What's so funny?"

"Mom, you just criticized me for not being able to hire help, and when I tell you I did, you criticize me for spending money on employees. What would you have me do differently?" I should have known better than to ask.

"Perhaps you could have started with some hourly help, asked your friends to pitch in a little, save some money."

I sighed. Only a tiny part of me wanted to tell her that's exactly what I had done, but I knew that would only lead to another, "Maybe you could have . . ." so I nodded. "You may be right, Mom."

I took a long swig of my latte and said, "Would you like a tour?"

For a moment, she smiled with her whole face, and I took a long, slow breath. My mother's critiques stemmed from her own perfectionism, not from her displeasure in me as her daughter. I didn't always remember that, but when I could, I was able to have a bit more compassion for her and a bit more patience, too. "I'd love that, Harvey."

For many years, my mom had tried to shake the nickname Dad had given me when I was about two. My given name was Anastasia Lovejoy Beckett, but somehow, Dad knew that I wasn't an Anastasia, not a Stacy either, even though that's what my friend Woody, the woodsmith, had taken to calling me as a joke. Mom hadn't liked it. Apparently, she'd suffered hard to find my given name and resented that my father stole it from me so quickly.

But finally, when I was in college, I'd told her that when she used my given name, she seemed like one of those persnickety people on TV shows who insisted on some fancy name and looked ridiculous, and she'd finally caved and started calling me Harvey. It felt like a major breakthrough in our relationship then, and it still does now, every time she says it.

I took her by the arm and walked her through each section of the store, pointed out the storeroom in the back and saw her take careful note of the security system with a nod, and then wove her back over to the café, where Dad and Daniel were in an intense conversation about Dodge Chargers.

A more polite person might have waited for a natural lull in the conversation, but I wasn't that person and simply waited until my dad took a breath to ask, "So how long are you guys staying? Headed back tonight?" Wishful thinking on my part.

"Oh, we're going to be in town for a couple of days at least. We saw all the wonderful things you advertised to do here and thought we'd take a few days of vacation here. One of the perks of retirement." Mom's voice was so casual that I braced myself. "Since your new assistant manager is starting tomorrow, maybe you can take the day off and show us around?"

The last thing I wanted to do – behind chewing on gravel, reading James Joyce's *Ulysses* (I hated that book), and eating raw oysters– was to give my parents a tour.

I must have looked panicked because Daniel quickly said, "Oh, man. I know you'd love to do that. But you have that whole training schedule for Marcus, don't you? I mean, maybe Mart could—"

"Dang. That's right. And Mart is away in Virginia consulting with that new winery outside Norfolk, so she can't take over." I had never been so glad Mart had a business trip as I was right now. "I'm afraid I can't give you a tour. But maybe we could all have dinner tonight, and we could make a plan for you all to be your own guides?"

My mother looked a bit crestfallen, and I almost felt guilty. I had no plan to train Marcus. He already knew everything, and while I had intended to be at the shop tomorrow just in case, I knew he'd have everything well in hand without me. But I wasn't about to let my mother know that.

I looked over my parents' heads to avoid making eye contact with them and saw Marcus and his mother, Josie, come into the shop. I waved, and they made their way over. I stood up and gave Josie a hug. She'd been writing a great review column for our newsletter, and like her son, she was part of what was growing our business. Plus, she was such a charming person.

"Marcus, Josie, please meet my parents, Sharon and Burt. Mom and Dad, Marcus is my new assistant manager, and this is his mother, Josie."

I saw it happening. The notching up of the charm as my dad shook first Marcus's hand and then Josie's. "It's a true pleasure to meet you both. Marcus, Harvey tells us that your first day is tomorrow."

When Marcus glanced over at me, I gave him a hard stare and hoped he knew that meant, "Just go with it."

"Yes, sir," Marcus said, turning back to my father. "I'm very honored to be working with your daughter. She's a great boss, and I love this shop."

Dad gave him a clap on the shoulder hard enough to rattle Marcus's thin frame. "Well, I'm glad you're giving her a hand. I'm sure after training you'll be fit as a fiddle."

Marcus flicked his eyes to me, and I could feel his mom looking at me, too, but they didn't betray a thing. "Yes, sir. I'm sure that's the case."

"Are you in town long?" Josie asked.

My mom put on her biggest smile. "Just a couple of days. We wanted to see what Harvey was up to here."

Daniel came over and took my hand. My mother wasn't lying – she really believed that's why they were here – but it still stung when clearly this was, yet again, about making her feel good, not about what would actually matter to me, even though she was saying it was entirely for me.

Josie looked at me, nodded, and turned back to my mother. "I know that Harvey and Marcus have a busy day here tomorrow, but I'm free. Would you like me to give you a tour of the area?"

I'm pretty sure my mouth actually fell open.

"That would be lovely, Josie. Thank you so much." My mom was practically melting. "I love this coat of yours," Mom said, taking the edge of Josie's emerald-green, wool coat between her fingers. Fashion was my mother's love language.

Dad stepped forward. "That's a very kind offer. Thank you. Should we meet you here? What time works for you?"

Josie turned to me and winked with the eye my parents couldn't see. "I think we should start with the most important place in St. Marin's, the bookstore. So let's meet here at ten for coffee, and then we'll begin the tour from here." She fluffed the back of her short stacked hair and smiled at me, her brown skin rosy around her cheeks.

I stood dumbfounded for a few seconds before I realized my parents were looking at me. "Oh, yes, that sounds great. Thank you, Ms. Dawson." I winked back at her and then said to my parents, "You'll have a lovely time, and we can meet for dinner."

"That'll be lovely dear," Mom said as she patted my arm and began to move toward the door. "I think we'll go to that charming little art place down the road. That is, if they're open."

"They're open." I could hear the edge in my voice. My mother had a way of making even the most serious work seem small if it wasn't done to her scale. "Cate, the director, is probably there herself. Should I call to ask if she can give you a behind-the-scenes tour?"

My dad stood up a bit taller. He was just as bad as my mom. Special treatment always felt like just what they deserved. "That would be wonderful. Thank you. Tell her we'll be there in ten minutes."

"I'll ask if she's available." I tried to not jab the phone out of my hands as I entered my passcode and opened the messaging app. Cate's reply was immediate. "I'd be thrilled to meet your parents."

"Don't be so sure about that," I mumbled, and Daniel gave my shoulders a quick squeeze.

"I'm headed that way. Why don't I walk you down?" Daniel said with a cheery lilt to his voice. Then, more quietly he whispered, "This way, I'll have a chance to warn Cate."

"Good thinking," I said as I hugged him quickly.

"See you for dinner at our place, Mom and Dad. Seven p.m. I'll cook."

My mom looked a little stricken, but I wasn't sure if it was because of the idea of eating at my house or eating my cooking. Either way, she couldn't do much about it now. If she refused, she'd look rude, and it was absolutely unthinkable for my mother to look rude.

She gave me another one of her stiff hugs, and they headed off with Daniel.

As soon as they were out the door, I turned to Josie. "Oh my word. How did you know?"

"Oh, woman, I know the look of parent fatigue and frustration when I see it. They seem like lovely people, but I expect they've failed you in some major way, given the number of times you sighed while they were here. They won't bother me nearly as much as they bother you, and we'll have a good time." She stepped forward and pulled me into a hug.

I felt tears pooling in my eyes. "Thank you."

"Marcus, that girl in the café looks like she needs a little loving, too, and I need a big ole cup of coffee. Besides, I think you and Harvey need to chat, right?"

I saw a flash of color run up Marcus's neck, but he nodded slightly. "I'll be over in a minute," he said.

I stepped in front of the register and leaned back against the counter. "What's up?"

"I really didn't want to bother you with this. I thought maybe I should just tell Sheriff Mason, but Mama thought I should run the information by you first."

"Alright." I stood upright, spread my legs apart, and put my hands on my hips. "I'm ready."

Marcus gave me a half-smile. "I know who the witness who identified me is."

I really stood up straight then. "You do? Who is it?"

He took a quick look around the shop. "Huckabee Harris's daughter, Miranda."

"Miranda Harris-Lewis put forth a false statement about her own father's death." I didn't know Miranda well. She and her twin daughters, Maisy and Daisy – their given names were worse than mine – had been in the shop a few times. She wasn't my favorite person – a little too prim and too demanding for my taste. She'd asked me to vacuum the floor around the small table and chairs we had in the children's section because there were crumbs. "I'm modeling good hygiene for my daughters, and I don't want them to think that it's acceptable for places of business to be filthy," she'd said. I had told her I'd get right on that, and then I'd purposefully forgotten for the rest of their visit.

On their second visit, she'd asked which of the books had just arrived. "I don't want the girls touching things that might be," she shivered, "covered in germs." I had assured her that I had personally sterilized every book in the store that morning, trying to make a joke out of a weird moment, and she'd thanked me profusely, not a hint of irony in her gratitude.

For their part, the girls were actually wonderful. They picked up after themselves and asked me great questions about the next books in their favorite series, *The Magic Treehouse*. I didn't think they loved the *entirely* pink, matching outfits their mother put them in – I had watched them slip a pair of glittery hairbows behind the picture books one day – but I can't say as I blame them for that.

Marcus nodded. "She did. Harriet, the office manager at the sheriff's office, and Mom are good friends. She let it slip."

I snickered. "And I bet Ms. Dawson had nothing to do with bringing about that little slip of the tongue."

"Nothing at all. Nope. No way." Marcus laughed. "I was as surprised as you. I don't even know that woman, I mean besides from the couple of times she was in here. Why would she try to implicate me in her father's murder? I mean doesn't she, maybe more than anybody, want the right person found?" His voice got a little high at the end.

"I suspect you were, sadly, the first person she thought of when she wanted to point the finger away from what really happened."

"Because I'm a black man."

I blew a puff of air out of my lips. "Yeah, probably so."

Marcus's muscles worked under his jaw, and I could tell he was angry, as he had every right to be. But he kept his cool. "So what do I do, Harvey? I don't think it will help to confront her. It would probably make things worse." He looked down at his shoes and then scuffed them against the carpet. "Do you think you could talk to her?"

I had been thinking that very thing. "Yep. I can totally do that. Let me think about how though, okay? Now, you need to go take that amazing mother of yours out for lunch, don't you think?"

I looked over at the café, and Rocky was laughing at something Josie was saying. It looked like Mama Dawson had struck again with just the right intervention.

3

I couldn't figure out what motivation Miranda Harris-Lewis would have for trying to frame Marcus, but I was determined to find out. I didn't like that she'd messed with my friend, and I could feel my curiosity carrying me away.

Sheriff Mason and Daniel both had warned me about sleuthing. The adage about curiosity and the cat had come up several times, but I couldn't seem to help myself. I was just one of those people who always had questions. I wanted to know the filming locations for every movie I loved. I had IMDB bookmarked so I could see who was married to whom on my favorite TV shows. And if I heard a word I didn't know, I went right to Dictionary.com to look it up. I hated unanswered questions, and I loved finding the answers. It was a delightful combination for a student and a useful one for a bookseller. It was, it turned out, a dangerous one for an amateur investigator.

Still, I couldn't be stopped, and I had a plan to figure out what Miranda Harris-Lewis was up to.

Thus far, the children's section in the shop was one of the most underutilized areas, and I really did want to change that. So I decided to solicit input from parents about what books and children's activities might interest their families.

I started with the parents I knew – namely Miranda Harris-Lewis – by sending out a FB message from our bookstore page asking for her input on our shop's children's programs. I had long ago learned that people love to be heard, and if you can give them a chance to give their perspective on something they know a lot about, they almost always jump at the chance. Miranda obviously knew a lot about her children and clearly was not shy about sharing her opinions, so I was hoping this tactic would work.

And it did. Fast. Miranda, Maisy, and Daisy were in the store before three p.m. I gave the girls a couple of the newest *Treehouse* books and set them up in the café with chocolate milk, asking Rocky to let us know if they needed anything. I expected they'd be just fine since they were already engrossed in the stories as their mom and I walked away.

Miranda was wearing jeans that I was fairly sure were ironed and a cardigan that looked so soft I had to resist touching, it both because that was weird and because I was certain my hands did not pass her standards of cleanliness. I felt pretty frumpy in my baggy jeans and knit-top that was supposed to be a dress for a much tinier person. Some days, I really did wish I cared about fashion.

We sat in the chairs by the psychology section, and she said, "I'm so honored to have been solicited for my perspective on your store. I see so much that can be, well, improved here."

I blinked a few times, took a deep breath, and said, "Thank you for coming in." Then, I steered the conversation to our specific focus and told her about our hopes to have regular children's programs – a total truth – and our desire to involve local parents and grandparents in our ordering plans – another truth. She nodded and smiled politely before she pulled a four-page, single-spaced list of book titles she recommended we carry out of her purse.

I stared at the pieces of paper for a long moment before I thought to say, "Thank you" again. The list was mostly books from the 1950s and '60s, some classics – *The Secret Garden* was on there – but a lot of obscure older books, titles I didn't even recognize and only knew the publication records of because Miranda had written each listing up as a full-on MLA citation, complete with publisher city, name, and date.

A lot of people are nostalgic about books. We like to give children the books we loved ourselves as children, but these books predated Miranda by about twenty-five years, so I was puzzled. Another question to ponder . . . but not my top priority today.

Suddenly – at least I hoped it seemed sudden – I threw my hand to my mouth and said, "Oh, Miranda. How insensitive of me." I stood up and put the papers on the chair behind me as I knelt beside her. "I can't believe I asked for your help with this on the day after your father died. I'm so callous and selfish." I took her hand in mine. "I hope you can forgive me. We can pick this up another time." I felt a little overdramatic. I had never in my life knelt at anyone's feet, but she seemed unfazed by my mediocre acting.

She gazed down at me and then gave me a bemused smile. "Oh, right. Don't worry about that. Dad and I weren't close."

You'd think that I, the woman who had just done everything she could to avoid spending a day with her own parents, would understand her perspective. But something about her tone gave me pause. It was too casual, maybe. At least I felt a little embarrassed about how much my parents infuriated me, but she was talking about her father with as much tenderness as she might

show for the person who took her toll payment on the Golden
Gate Bridge.

I stood up and said, "Oh. Okay. Well, then." I was very articulate
when I was befuddled. But then I took a deep breath, sat back
down, and realized I probably didn't need to tread so lightly
after all. "Still, I was sorry to hear he died." I lowered my voice
like I was a bit embarrassed by my nosiness and said, "Forgive
me asking, but how did he die?"

She said, at full volume, "He was murdered. They think it was
poison in his nicotine gum. He was always chewing the stupid
stuff, so it wouldn't have been too hard to get it into him, I
guess." She was adjusting the pink bows on her jeans, trying to
make them symmetrical, but it still sounded like she was talking
about what she had for dinner last night.

"Oh, poison. Gracious. I mean, I don't know much about
murder, but don't they say that poison is what women use to
commit murder and wouldn't someone have to get pretty close
to your dad to get poison in his gum? "

She looked up at me then, but not with concern, more with
piqued curiosity. "Is that what they say? On TV? Or is that an
actual police practice?"

I didn't know how to answer her question, not only because it
seemed like a strange thing to ask when someone had just
suggested that your father was murdered by someone he knew
. . . but also because I didn't know the actual answer. I had
picked up a fair amount of my knowledge about murder and
murder investigations from TV shows, as the sheriff had noted,
so I wasn't that confident of my statement. But she didn't know
that. "Police lore. A friend of mine who is a profiler mentioned
it."

Now, she was more than just curious. She was downright enthusiastic. "You have a friend who's a profiler? Like on *Criminal*

Minds? Do they live here? Can I meet them?" Her knees were bouncing, and she had moved to the edge of her seat.

"Um, well, she likes to keep a low profile. I probably shouldn't have said anything." Darn right, I shouldn't have said anything. I shouldn't have lied, and then I shouldn't have compounded the lie with another lie. "Anyway, do you think someone who knew your dad poisoned him?"

It took her a minute to answer, like she was trying to pay attention to what I was actually saying, but eventually, she said, "What, oh no. That kid who works here killed him."

Well, that got us right to the point. "What kid who works here?"

"You know, the black one."

I sat perfectly still and just stared at her for a minute while she picked an invisible something off her sweater. I was dumbfounded. She had just called another person, a person I cared about, "the black one." I wanted to ask her to leave my store, but only after I had a long talk with her daughters about how Mommy was a racist.

I needed to get answers for Marcus. though, so instead, I gathered my thoughts and said, "You mean Marcus Dawson, my assistant manager? I would appreciate it you would refer to him as Mr. Dawson from now on."

Her eyes darted up to mine, and she gave her head a little shake. "Well, he is black, isn't he?"

"He is. But he's a person, a black person, but a full person who is not simply defined by—"

"Whatever," she interrupted. "He did it. I saw him there."

I just kept staring at this woman as she lied directly to my face, but I felt something wheedling at the back of my mind. I couldn't grab it through my anger though.

"So you're the witness?" I was done playing games and trying to be nice with this woman. "The one who lied and told the police that Marcus was at the farm stand yesterday afternoon."

She sucked in a quick breath as she glared at me. "Did you just say I lied?" She looked angry, but her voice shook.

"I did." I kept my voice even and quiet, but all of me wanted to stand up and announce that this very put-together woman was overtly racist. "Marcus was here in the store all afternoon. Several dozen people saw him and interacted with him. He was nowhere near Elle Heron's store at the time you claim."

I watched her carefully check her purse and then stand before she walked over to my chair and glowered down at me. "I know what I saw." She turned and motioned to her daughters, who quickly set their books neatly on the table and headed toward the front door. Then, Miranda turned back to me. "Don't you ever accuse me of doing something as crass as lying again. Ever. You wouldn't like me when I am angry."

Then she spun on a heel and led her daughters out the front door. They each waved as they left, looking a little forlorn.

I didn't quite know what to make of that last statement, but it had set my hands shaking – from rage and maybe from a little fear – so I decided it was fair to think of it as a threat. Miranda Harris-Lewis had just threatened me. Before I could talk myself out of it, I picked up the phone and called the police station. I didn't want to alarm anyone. I didn't think I was in imminent danger, but I did think it might be useful for the sheriff to know what happened.

He was out, but Harriet, the dispatcher, told me she'd ask him to stop by as soon as possible. I thanked her and then tried to stay busy.

Fortunately, the stream of customers was steady for the rest of the day, and I was able to pour myself into book recommendations and ringing up sales. In the few lulls we had, I worked on the week's newsletter. I was excited to announce the new Staff Recommendations shelf we were adding with books from everyone who worked here. I knew from my own experience that I loved finding a great book on a staff picks' shelf and then seeing if that person was working so I could tell them I was going to try the book or that I loved it too. The booksellers I'd talked to had always seemed genuinely excited to talk about their favorites with customers, and I hoped our own shelf would help us get to know more of the folks who came to All Booked Up.

We were each starting with one book. My pick was *The Cloister Walk* by Kathleen Norris, and Rocky had chosen *Home Front* by Kristin Hannah. Mart had selected *An American Marriage* by Tayari Jones, and Marcus had introduced me to a fantasy title, *Senlin Ascends* by Josiah Bancroft. It was a wide variety of books, and I loved that. I thought our customers might, too.

All in all, the sales day was good – not ridiculously good, but steady, and I'd take steady. Steady was what paid the bills. When closing time came around, I was satisfied with the day and ready to relax. I even, almost, looked forward to cooking for my parents. I'd decided that we'd go very casual – breakfast for dinner. Since they hadn't given me any warning they'd be in touch and since I'd decided to agitate them a bit by insisting I cook for them, I was left with what was available. I always had bacon and eggs available.

Daniel met me, as usual, at the shop door as I closed up for the evening, and he, Mayhem, Taco, and I walked home with a little more speed than usual. I knew Mom and Dad would be waiting. I'd texted Dad to remind him that the shop closed at seven, so I'd be home soon after, but I knew they'd be on my step with sour faces if I was more than a few minutes late.

So I was pleasantly surprised and then immediately worried when we got there and they hadn't yet arrived. My first impulse was to text them and ask if they were okay, but I figured that if they were in trouble, someone in town would have let me know.

I got out the griddle and put the bacon on. Then, I whipped up a batch of from-scratch pancake batter since I had a little extra time. I was just flipping the last pancake and pouring out the scrambled eggs when there was a knock at the door.

Daniel set his beer down on the counter and went to answer it while the two-dog alarm went off at a deafening level. Our dogs would surely lick someone to death before they'd bite, but I was confident that no one intending harm would even want to come through that door and into all the racket.

Mom and Dad came in with big smiles on their faces, and I almost felt relieved. Almost. There was something odd about the way Dad was looking at me, something mischievous.

Then, I saw Sheriff Mason coming up behind them and understood. My dad thought he'd made a special friend and would get to introduce me to the important man in town, the highest law enforcement officer in the land. This was going to be fun.

"Sheriff Mason, oh, I'm so glad to see you." I went over and gave him a big hug, which clearly took him by surprise since he jolted when I grabbed him. "You must have gotten my message," I said as I stepped back.

He gave me a puzzled look but then said, "I did. Then, when I met these two fine folks who mentioned they were the parents of the new bookstore owner, I thought I'd take the opportunity to spend time with the parents of one of my favorite people AND follow up on your call."

I think my face practically broke open with delight when I saw my father look from the sheriff to me and back to the sheriff. "So you two know each other then?" he said.

"We do," I said. "Pretty well, in fact. We worked on, um, a project together when the shop first opened." I smiled at the sheriff. "Let's go into the living room to talk." I caught Daniel's eye and saw he was trying hard not to laugh himself. "Mind finishing up the eggs?"

"Happy to," he said, and I gave him a quick kiss on the cheek as I handed him the spatula and said, "Catch you up later."

He smiled and turned to the stove. My parents stood by the counter for a minute, clearly confused about what was happening, but then began to take off their coats and look around. Judging our house would keep them busy for a while.

THE SHERIFF and I sat on the couch on the other side of the living room from the kitchen. It wasn't exactly private since the main living space had an open floor plan, but at least we could talk without direct intervention from my parents. The significant looks, however, passed right to me.

The sheriff looked at me intently and said, "So Miranda threatened you?"

When he put it like that, I felt a little silly. "Well, sort of, I mean she said that I shouldn't call her a liar if I knew what was good for me."

The sheriff cleared his throat. "You called her a liar? To her face?"

I relayed the conversation, including Miranda's racist commentary, and by the end of my story, the sheriff was nodding. "I'd say that calling her a liar was the kindest of the available and fitting options for titles."

"You know her?"

"I do." He looked out the front window into the gathering dusk before he straightened his posture. "She has, well, some issues. Unfortunately, she often comes across much like her father. I suspect he tried to teach her to hold her ground." I sensed there was a lot more to this choice of words, but I had other things to think about, like solving a murder and putting my friend Elle's mind at ease about her lack of action.

I nodded. "Yeah, I could see that. Even directly confronted about her lie, she doubled-down. She's ridiculous, that's for sure, but I don't know. I didn't get the murderer vibe."

Sheriff Mason let out a sharp, hoarse laugh. "The murderer vibe? What, are you a psychic now?"

"What's all this talk about murder?" My mom had come into the room silently, like a cat, and I almost jumped when she spoke.

She was peering at me with a feigned, wide-eyed expression, but I knew that look – that expression coupled with patient silence could make almost anyone tell her anything. But I was wise to her game.

My first instinct was to try and make up some story about a TV show, but given that I'd just accused someone of lying, I didn't think it flattering to do so myself. Besides, I'd already told a couple of tales in the past two days. But I didn't really relish my mother's involvement in this situation.

"We were just talking about an unfortunate death here in town, Mrs. Beckett. Harvey is a good sounding board." The sheriff shot my mother a smile that would have won over the heart of Clint Eastwood's gruffest character.

Mom shot me a glance and then smiled at the sheriff. "Well, isn't that interesting? I didn't realize the police involved civilians in their investigations."

And there it was – the zinger coated in feigned ignorance. My mother was not someone who liked to be left outside of anything – not social gatherings, not fashion trends, and definitely not gossip. But if I was in, and she was out, that was even worse. She loved me, of course, but she always thought I was a little out of it, a little bedraggled and wild. For years when I was a child, she'd tried to groom me, get me to care more about my appearance and my choice in clothing. When I'd entered my teenage years and suddenly developed opinions about fashion, I think she thought she might have a chance, but Eddie Vedder and the grunge scene dashed all her hopes. I was on trend and in flannel. I was living my best life, which happened to be her worst nightmare.

The sheriff's smile only faltered for a split second before he said, "Oh we don't." He shot me a quick look, and I nodded slightly. "But since Harvey found the body, I do need to discuss the case with her. Now, if you'll excuse us, this is an open investigation, so I need to ask for the room."

I had always loved the expression "I'll need the room" and to have it employed against my nosy, snobbish mother made me ecstatic.

She pursed her lips and looked at me. I gave her a "What can I do?" shrug, and she literally spun on her heel and walked back into the kitchen.

I whispered, "Sorry. She can be a little much."

"You think that's *much*?" Sheriff Mason said with a grin. "My mother can insult you while she hands you a pie, and you won't even know it until your second slice."

I guffawed, and my mother's head whipped around to look at us again.

With a quick throat-clearing, I got myself back under control. "What do you think? Is Miranda a suspect?"

The sheriff's mood quickly returned to somber. "I doubt it. She's hard to deal with, but I don't know that she'd have any reason to murder her father. I'll look into it though."

I walked the sheriff to the door. "Maybe you could talk to Marcus – a little man talk."

"I had already planned on it. Black man to black man. This uniform doesn't mean I haven't been falsely accused of lots of things because people are scared of black men." He stepped through the front door and turned back. "I'll stop by there now. Just to check on him."

"Thanks, Sheriff. See you soon?"

"Most people don't want the police coming around, Harvey."

"Well, I'm not most people, am I?" I gave him a wink as I closed the door.

As I walked back into the kitchen, the conversation stopped, and everyone turned to look at me. My father was curious, Daniel, too, but my mother looked out-and-out angry.

"You found a body, Anastasia? A dead body? What kind of places are you spending your time that you come across a body?"

I knew that when my mother took out my given name I should be wary, but her implication that people only died places she deemed "despicable" was both absurd and ignorant.

"At the local farm stand, Mother. I found his body at my friend Elle's farm stand." As soon as Elle's name came out of my mouth, I regretted it. I didn't need to subject my friend to my mother's judgments.

But my mom pulled her chin back slightly and let out a long breath. "Someone died in that lovely little farm place up the street from your shop? How awful. We stopped in there today and talked with the owner – Elle, did you say her name was? She was delightful and gave me the best tips about my lilac bushes." Mom looked at me again. "I do hope this doesn't hurt her business."

I decided not to be petty and point out that my mother had expressed no such concerns when I'd found a body in my own shop. Instead, I let out a long sigh and said, "I don't think it will. The sheriff is very discrete about these matters. Local people will know, of course, but then local people also know Elle and her wares. I don't think she'll suffer. She may even get a little extra foot traffic thanks to the gossip."

This conjecture seemed to lift my mother's spirits. She pulled out a chair at the dining room table and smiled at me. "Harvey, would you mind if your father poured us some drinks?"

I was dumbfounded that my mother had actually asked permission to do something in my home. It wasn't her style to ask for anything, but when I looked at her and saw the anxiousness on her face, I softened. She was trying. "Of course. We don't have a lot, Dad, but over there in that corner cabinet, you'll find the essentials."

Dad took our drink orders – a Cosmo for my mom, a Whiskey Sour for Daniel, and a Dirty Martini with extra olives for me. After making our drinks, Dad poured himself a Vodka Collins and served us from a little round tray that I didn't even know we owned. I was wary about using alcohol to manage anything, but tonight, it seemed that the mixing of a bit of spirits was lifting our own and the tension along with them.

Dinner was quiet and enjoyable. I don't know many people who don't enjoy breakfast for dinner. Then, for dessert, I whipped up instant vanilla pudding, dolloped on fresh whipped cream that I made from the cream I'd picked up the day before from Elle's shop, and sprinkled on some fresh raspberries. It wasn't fancy, but it sure was delicious.

After dinner, Dad made us another round of drinks, and we sat around our living room in a sort of satiated casualness. I leaned back into the crook of Daniel's arm and felt myself start to relax.

But then my mother said, "I didn't know whether to tell the sheriff this, but earlier today, I overheard two men talking about some land that was now available. It sounded like they were both interested in it because someone had been unwilling to sell until now."

I wasn't sure where this was going, but my mother was quite intelligent. If she thought something warranted attention, it probably did.

"I didn't think anything of it until I heard someone had died. Was the victim, by chance, a farmer?"

That got my attention. "Yes, a dairy farmer in fact. Why?"

"So they were talking about the man who died then." Mom looked out the window for a moment and then returned her gaze to me. "They were saying that the farmer had been sitting on his land acting like a king of his castle and lording his wealth over everyone. They were hoping the farmer's daughter didn't know the value of what was– excuse my language here – 'under all that cow shit.' I got the impression they were going to try to buy the land for far less than they thought it was worth."

"Did they say anything more about what was so valuable? I mean good agricultural land can be very—"

Mom shook her head. "No, I got the impression that whatever it was, was sizable and quick. Something that could be dug up, maybe, and sold."

I looked at Daniel, and he said, "I have no idea. I haven't heard anything, but then, I wouldn't, right? No one is going to talk about buried treasure with a local who might go get it themselves. Good sleuthing, Mrs. B."

Mom fairly beamed at Daniel's words, but I couldn't tell if she was happy because of the praise or because of the nickname. Mom was a big fan of nicknames. She was always giving them out, even to people she barely knew. It was her form of an icebreaker, I guess.

I didn't really care about why she was happy though. She seemed to like Daniel, and while I didn't need her approval, it certainly made things easier and more pleasant.

"Can you describe these two men, Mom?"

She looked at my father, and I watched a very familiar expression come over his face. My dad had as much penchant for the details of someone's physical appearance as my mother did for social hierarchies. He could remember what someone was wearing on the day in third grade when he'd figured out he could sell chocolate milk to his classmates at a premium if he bought all that was available early in the day and then controlled the supply at lunchtime.

"Two men. One white. One black. Looked to be about fifty-five or sixty. Slim. Fit but not muscle-bound. If I had to guess, I'd think they played a lot of golf and passed on the carts. The white man had a wide moustache that twirled up at the ends, and the black man was mostly bald with a slight tonsure of hair just above his ears."

"Pickle and Bear," Daniel said.

"Excuse me?" My mother leaned forward. "Are you still hungry, dear? Did you just ask for a pickle?"

Daniel grinned. "No, ma'am. Those two men. Their nicknames are Pickle and Bear. Pickle Herring and Bear Johnson."

My dad almost spit out his drink. "Pickle Herring? I guess we know why he has that nickname."

"Yep. And Bear gets his from some exaggerated legend about him wrestling a bear when it came after him on a hike one day. I've always imagined the bear was a tiny cub, but who knows? Bear is a pretty unintimidating guy, if you ask me."

"You're sure that's who Dad described." I sat forward and looked back at him on the couch behind me.

"Yep, the moustache is a giveaway, and those two are thick as thieves. Always together. Plus, it makes sense they'd be at the co-op. Bear's wife has a studio there. I think you met her, Harvey. Henry Johnson?" Daniel asked.

"Oh, Henry. Yes, I love her, and her work is so beautiful. Mom, you must have noticed it. She's a weaver. Makes these lush table runners and wall hangings."

"Notice her. I bought one of her pieces. Plan on hanging it in the —" She stopped short and looked at Dad before looking back at me with a big smile. "In the house."

I smiled back and tried to hold off asking any questions about that odd moment. The night was going well, and I loved that Mom had bought one of Henry's pieces. My mom had always been a great supporter of the arts, but even more than that, she liked to support under-noticed artists. I did love that about her. "Can't wait to see it."

"I'll bring it when we come to pick you up for dinner tomorrow.

Pick you – and you, too, Daniel – up at the shop at seven tomorrow?"

Daniel gave me a glance, and after I nodded, he said, "Sounds great. See you then."

Mom and Dad stood, put on their coats and headed to the door, where she turned and looked back at me. "This was lovely, Harvey. Thank you for a relaxing, comfortable evening."

I smiled even as I braced for the lash that often came after my mother's compliments, but she just turned and walked out the door on Dad's arm.

"You did it," Daniel said as we watched their headlights move back up the drive. "She's a feisty one, your mom, but I like her."

I gazed at this man in my life and felt almost overcome with gratitude. He saw me, saw how I reacted to my mom, respected that, and still knew I really wanted him to like her. I was a lucky woman.

I WAS a lucky woman who needed to tell the sheriff about this mysterious "treasure" buried at Harris's farm. But first, I needed more intel. Good thing my new assistant manager started the next morning.

———

4

*T*he next morning, Marcus was, unsurprisingly, right on time, and it looked like his mom had taken him shopping. He was wearing crisp blue jeans, a carefully ironed blue button-down, and some very cool Air Jordans in a hot blue. "Looking fly," I said tentatively when he came in behind me that morning.

He snickered and said, "Two things, Ms. B. The word *fly* went out about ten years ago, and also, it's not a good look on you."

"Noted," I said with a laugh. I had this obsessive need to seem cool and hip, but I should have learned that my desire to seem cool and hip always had the opposite effect in that regard. "Don't ask me about the time I tried out, 'Let's bounce!' on my dad."

"You did not?"

I gave him a quick nod before I headed to the café for the morning caffeine.

A quick ring of the bell told me someone had come in, and when I walked back with two of Rocky's largest cups, I saw Woody talking with Marcus by the register. "Hi Woody. What brings you in?"

"Nothing much. Just here to congratulate Marcus on his first day."

I smiled. Woody had taken a liking to Marcus from the get-go, had even made it his mission to get Marcus into woodworking. I can't say as the bookish young man I knew was much into whittling and lathes, but he was respectful and enjoyed spending time with Woody. So he took the lessons as the cost of making a new friend.

"That's nice of you, Woody. Can I get you a cup of coffee?"

"No, thank you. Already had two cups. Can't manage more than that, if you know what I mean."

I had no idea what he meant, but I thought I probably preferred it that way. "Got it. I have a question for you since you're here." I handed Marcus his coffee and leaned back against a stool. "You ever hear anything about Huckabee Harris's farm? I mean about something valuable being out there?"

"Nothing unusual that I can think of. Why do you ask?"

I told him quickly about what Mom had overheard Pickle and Bear talking about. "So I was just wondering. Maybe that's why he was killed?" I asked.

"I wouldn't put too much credence in what Pickle and Bear say. Those boys fancy themselves venture capitalists. Always looking for the next get-rich-quick scheme. One time, they invested in a vineyard that they saw on the internet. Went around town bragging they were going to be the owners of a famous wine-making enterprise soon. Turned out, they'd bought into an illegal moonshine operation up in Cecil County. Had to do some fast talking with the sheriff to get out of that one. Those boys are very smart men, just not always wise with their cash, if you know what I mean."

With names like Pickle and Bear, I didn't doubt it. "Still, makes me wonder."

Woody shot Marcus a glance. "She's getting curious again, isn't she?"

"Yes, sir. I believe she is. I'd try to stop her, but I know there's no use."

"None at all." Woody gave me a sideways look. "What do you say I take you out to Harris's place this afternoon? I need to pick up a few slabs of wood that he sold me a while back and never delivered. You can poke around, and I can keep you from getting into trouble."

Apparently, I had a reputation. "I'd love the escort, Woody. Marcus, you can hold down the fort after lunch, I expect?"

"Sure thing, Ms. B."

And just like that, I was going on a treasure hunt, and I hadn't even had to make up my own excuse to start it.

MARCUS and I spent the morning making sure he was up to speed on the management systems of the shop. He'd already done most everything, but now he had managerial access to the computers and needed to be taught how to read the reports and things. He caught on quickly, and while I'd had no doubt I'd made a good choice to hire him, I was especially pleased when he looked forlorn over the pick list, the sheet that I printed out each week that told us what books had been here for over a month without a single sale. I couldn't afford to keep stock that wasn't selling – it took up space that might actually go to a book that generated some revenue – and so the pick list was what we used to put together our returns to the publisher.

"I hate returning books, Ms. B," Marcus said as he looked at the list. "Someone worked really hard to write that book, and it just sucks that we have to send it back. They lose the money then, right?"

I sighed. "They do. I hate it, too. But see this binder? I started it the first week the shop was open. It's got a list of every book I've returned, and each week that I have a little extra revenue, I go back in and reorder one of those books. Get that author that sale again."

"Do any of them ever sell the second time?"

"A couple have because I work hard to display them well or recommend them to folks."

Marcus picked up the binder. "Mind if I take this to lunch with me? I'd like to study up so I can read these titles and recommend them to people."

I smiled. This guy's heart and endless reading appetite gave me joy. "Feel free."

Marcus headed out the door, the orange binder tucked under his arm, and I spent the next hour tidying the shelves and pondering a new window display of "Second Chance Books" compiled from the pick list. I'd have to get Marcus to recommend his favorites, and maybe we could get some of those works of art into homes.

Woody arrived right at one, just as Marcus came in from lunch. My assistant manager assured me that he was all set with the store and that he'd text if he needed me, and I left, feeling care-free and eager to explore with Woody. Plus, it was an amazing spring day, and I hadn't had much more than an afternoon here and there off since the shop opened. It felt good to get out into the world for a bit.

I hadn't paid much attention to Woody's vehicle (Daniel was very precise with his language about, um, vehicles: "Not everything is a car, Harvey.") before, but somehow it fit perfectly that he drove a beat-up pick-up with a tailgate whose paint didn't match the rest of the car. It wasn't a honking monstrosity of a truck either, which I appreciated since I didn't fancy using a trampoline to get into the passenger's seat.

As I climbed in, I saw a wide-ranging assortment of ratchet straps and bungee cords mixed in with what appeared to be fifteen years' worth of Styrofoam coffee cups and plastic bags behind the seat. I was hoping the jack and lug wrench weren't buried in there because from the looks of the truck, it could be that we might need to change a tire . . . or two.

Woody and I made small talk on the way over. I caught him up on how business was going, and he told me about the new piece he was working on – a slab of maple that he was fashioning into a large table. "It could be for a really big dining room or for some corporate board room. All I'm saying is that this isn't your 'I work a normal job' type of table."

I laughed. "So you don't think it would work at my house? That's what you're telling me."

Woody gave me a sideways grin. "That's exactly what I'm telling you, dear. Exactly."

When we pulled up to a large black gate, I turned to Woody in confusion. "Are you stopping to drop off that table?"

"Nope. This is Huckabee Harris's place. Plenty snazzy for a farmer, huh?"

"I'll say." I mean, I don't know that much about farms, but I didn't expect an electronic gate surrounded by landscaping that was, obviously, tended by gardeners what with the freshly mulched beds and the perfectly symmetrical tulip groupings.

Woody leaned over and spoke into an intercom. Then, the gate – as if by magic – swung open to let us in.

"Aren't you just the powerful one?"

"If you count being able to repair your hand-crafted bannister before someone breaks their neck, then yes, I am powerful." He grinned. "Actually, I just know the caretaker, Homer Sloan. He's a friend."

I nodded and took in the view of the pristine white farmhouse with its four brick chimneys and half a dozen outbuildings set in front of a vast pasture dotted with black and white cows. As we approached the house, I got a glimpse into the red barn, which was loaded full of green tractors and implements. I had no idea what those big machines cost, but I bet it was more than my car, maybe my car and my house put together. Harris must have done alright for himself as a farmer.

On the front porch, a slim man with a long, dark beard waited for us. We climbed out and met him on the steps. "Homer, this is Harvey. Harvey, Homer."

"Nice to meet you, Harvey," he said as he gave my hand a hearty handshake. "Woody here tells me you've heard the rumors of treasure, too."

I shrugged. "The rumor did reach me, but I'm not really interested in finding it – unless there's a sizeable finder's fee, of course. Then, I'm all in."

Homer threw back his head and laughed. "Woody said you were a witty girl, and he's right." He looked out over the lawn in front of the house. "Well, if you're not here for the treasure, how can I help you?"

"Just came to get that wood Huck had for me. Mind if I grab it from the barn while you two get to know each other?" Woody shot me a quick wink.

"No problem at all. It's in that little garage over there by my truck. Need a hand lifting it?"

"Nope. I'll use this as my excuse for a nap later." He climbed back in among the coffee cups and drove the couple hundred feet to the one-stall garage that looked like it might have once held a wagon.

Homer smiled at me. "You just fancied a day out in the country?"

I laughed. "I do appreciate the farmland out here, but I did actually have a couple of questions about that supposed treasure." He gave me a puzzled look, and I explained about Pickle and Bear's theory.

"Those two wouldn't know a treasure if it shined itself up and put itself in their wallets." He gestured toward the barn and started walking. Woody pulled up beside us, shut off the truck, and joined us.

As we strolled down the gravel lane, Homer said, "Somewhere back in the day, somebody started a rumor about Confederate gold hidden here in the barn."

Woody groaned. "If the Confederates had actually had all the gold people claimed was hidden under floorboards and in attics, they'd have been able to buy the Federal government right out from under Lincoln's rear."

"Sure glad they didn't." Homer said with a heavy tone. "But you're right. Most old places in the South have some rumor of Confederate gold attached to them. But that's all they are: rumors. I've cleaned out every building on this place, pulled up most of the floor boards to fix pipes, too. There's no hidden gold here."

I let my eyes take in the size and beauty of the dairy barn. A two-story structure with wide doors on a center aisle and what looked to be a hayloft above. I could see how it might seem reasonable that things were stashed in all these outbuildings, but if Homer had gone through them and not found anything, and if that was common knowledge, as Homer seemed to imply it was, then Pickle and Bear couldn't have been thinking they'd strike it rich from some sort of trove of gold bars. "Alright, then, could they have been thinking of some other kind of treasure? Maybe some family jewels or something buried in the fields?" I realized I was sounding a bit like an adventure novel, but something was telling me that this wasn't some far-flung hope that was driving Pickle and Bear.

"No family jewels except the, er, anatomical ones," Homer gave me an awkward grin, but when I started to giggle, he let out a roar that startled the starlings out of the barn eaves. When he got his breath, he said, "I can't think of anything that is hidden here. Obviously, Huck had some wealth, but that was no secret. He flaunted his cash with abandon, and anything he didn't tote around for show was kept in a safe as big as your car that sits plain as day in his office. He wasn't trying to hide some secret stash."

I looked around at the immaculate farmyard and poked my head into the barn door to see two of the largest tractors I'd ever seen, each with a cab that Homer told me had satellite radio and was climate-controlled. I could see what he meant about Harris not being afraid to flaunt his cash.

I sighed as we walked back toward the house. Woody heard me and looked over. "Don't worry, Harvey. Something will come clear eventually. Besides, it's just as well. Daniel would rather you weren't sleuthing around anyway."

I knew my, um, boyfriend didn't like when I investigated, but curiosity always won with me. It was one of my biggest strengths and also a distinct character flaw.

As we all leaned up against Woody's truck, I asked the obvious question. "So Huckabee Harris made all this money from dairy cows?"

Homer's laugh could have cracked open the sky. "Oh no. No, no, no. This is oil money, Ms. Beckett. 'Black gold. Texas tea.'" He pointed across the pasture, and there, beyond the cattle, was an oil rig, its hammerhead top going up and down rhythmically.

"He was mining oil? Does one *mine* oil? I mean, there's oil here?"

"Yep, a lot of it apparently. Huck drilled a water well once and came upon the stuff. Apparently, there's a pretty big deposit here. So while he could, he bought up all the land around and started wells."

I looked hard at Woody and then at Homer, and they gazed back at me sweetly, but clearly without a clue. "Seriously, guys. Don't you think this is what Pickle and Bear were talking about?"

The men looked at each other and then shrugged almost in unison. "Could be, I guess. Just sounded like it was some kind of secret thing, the way you described it. Most everybody, I mean everybody who's lived here for a little while," Woody blushed, "knew about Huck's wells. Pickle and Bear definitely knew. So that didn't sound like what you were describing, Harvey. Now you think it is, though?"

"From the looks of this place, I'd say there's enough oil here to motivate the right person to murder, don't you think?"

"Probably so," Homer said as he looked out across the fields. "But then, of course, that's where Miranda would be the biggest hurdle. She's the heir."

I walked around to the back of Woody's truck, wrenched down the tailgate, and hopped up on it. I had never in my life done such a thing and felt a little self-conscious, but the two men didn't act as if I'd done anything odd at all. They just leaned against the sides of the truck and looked at me.

"I didn't think Miranda and her dad got along." I almost added, *That's what Miranda said*, but I didn't. Better to tell too little than reveal all my secrets.

"Oh, they didn't. But Huck still loved that girl. She didn't come around much anymore." Homer's voice had gone soft, and his eyes were fixed on a point out in his memory. "But he still loved her. Left her everything. Even put together a huge trust for those twin grandbabies, but she kept her distance. She had her reasons."

"Miranda Harris-Lewis has some motive then."

Homer looked me straight in the eye and said, "Yes. Yes she does."

THE RIDE back to town was pretty quiet. My mind was spinning with possibilities. Miranda clearly had motive, and she'd lied about seeing Marcus at the crime scene. Pickle and Bear definitely had motive, too, if they could find some way to get their hands on the oil or the oil proceeds. But then, everyone in town, except me apparently, knew about the oil, so that opened up the range of suspects pretty wide. I kept running through the possible murderers and not getting any further. I just didn't have enough information.

We pulled up to the shop, and Woody switched off the truck and turned to me. "I can feel the heat from your brain working all the way over here, Harvey. I know you can't help yourself, but please, can you promise not to do anything ridiculous or haphazard as you follow your curiosity?"

I looked over at my friend, and then put my hand over his on the seat between us. "Yes, Woody. I will not do anything ridiculous or haphazard, okay?"

"By my definition of those terms, young lady. Not yours."

I laughed. He had a point. "Deal." I opened my door. "Thank you for the ride. I liked spending the afternoon with you."

"Back at ya, kiddo," he said. I slammed the door, and he pulled out.

I must have been smiling because when I turned around, I heard my worst nightmare say, "It's not bad enough that you blew off your own parents on their one full day in town, but you come back grinning like the cat who ate the canary. I'm disappointed in you, Anastasia."

I had frozen in place when my mother started talking, and I had one foot on the curb and one still in the street. I was staring right at her, but I could not make words come out of my mouth. She was right, but there was no way I was going to tell her that. I'd never hear the end of her gloating. So I opted for ignoring her. Well, not her, but her words.

"Oh hi, Mom. I thought we were meeting at seven. Did you need something?" I smiled and resumed my approach to the shop door.

Mom then stepped in front of me. "I demand you tell me where you were. You said you couldn't—"

I didn't let her finish. "Mom, it's been over twenty years since you had the right to demand to know my whereabouts." I opened the door to the shop and let it shut behind me as I stalked to the backroom, where I closed the door and locked it while I gathered my temper. I couldn't believe I had just said that to my mother, but the nerve of her. She had shown up unannounced, expected me to drop everything for her, and then had the audacity to challenge me about how I spent my time.

I had a pretty good righteous tizzy going until I realized that she was right, at least in one sense. I had lied to her. I had tried to avoid an awkward conversation with a lie, and now here I was with a full-blown conflict . . . and my mother's hurt feelings. Righteous indignation disappears quickly when you realize you're in the wrong.

I took a deep breath and was just heading to open the door when someone knocked. "Ms. B, it's me. I'm so sorry. I should have texted you to let you know that Mom brought them by for coffee and so she could brag about you a little bit. She didn't know you'd be gone—"

I opened the door and looked at Marcus. His face was drawn with worry. "I know, Marcus. How could she? Your mom is so sweet to spend the day with my parents, and here, I've put you all in an awkward spot." I let out a hard breath. "Let's go up front, and I'll get this all straightened out. Don't you worry." I put my hand on his back and rubbed small circles.

When we got to the register, my mother was there with her head on my dad's chest, and Josie was wringing the life out of scarf. All three of them opened their mouths to speak, but I raised my hand over my head, palm up, and they each stopped.

"Mom and Dad, I owe you an apology. I should have simply told you that I wanted to spend at least part of my day at the shop and that I was a bit put out by you showing up here unannounced and expecting me to drop everything. I do appreciate you coming to visit though."

I turned to Josie then, leaving my parents to react however they would. "Ms. Dawson, I'm so sorry my lack of forthrightness made for this awkward moment. Thank you so much for taking my parents around St. Marin's and showing off my work here in the shop in a way that I was afraid to do. You are a good friend."

Finally, I looked at Marcus. "You have done a stellar job on this your first day as assistant manager, Marcus, and I put you in a terrible position. I'm so sorry. Thank you for wanting so badly to make things right."

I then looked at each of them and waited. Marcus raised a hand and gave me a high five before sliding behind the register. Josie kissed me on the cheek and then walked into the café. Mom and Dad looked at each other and then at me. I didn't know what to expect. I had a slim dream that they might say they understood, that they were sad I couldn't talk to them openly, and that while they were hurt that I lied, they would try to do better.

Instead, my mother looked me in the eye and said, "I can see that your juvenile investigatory instincts are more important than your parents' valuable time. We'll be going back to Baltimore now. You can come see us when your schedule permits."

Then, she turned around and walked right out the front door, leaving Dad standing with his arm still in the position that he'd held her in. He gave me a shrug and followed her out.

I kind of wanted to cry, but I'd been the brunt of my mother's overblown anger far too often to be able to get very worked up over it now. I'd apologized. I'd tried to empathize with her feelings. She just simply was not capable of trying to understand mine. I didn't like that, but I could do nothing to change it – goodness knows I'd tried my whole life – so I took a shuddering breath and went to straighten up the romance section. All those happily-ever-afters had to give me hope, didn't they?

At seven, I turned off the neon OPEN sign, thanked Marcus and

Rocky for another great day, and waved Daniel inside. Taco trotted in ahead of him as usual and sniffed out Mayhem over in the psychology section.

I took out the bottle of Chimay that I was gifted by a grateful book buyer a few weeks earlier and that had never made it home, grabbed two coffee mugs from the café, and pointed to the chairs in the fiction section. Daniel looked puzzled, but he took a seat, accepted the mug I handed him, and let me fill it up. I filled my own mug and dropped into the chair across from him.

"So no dinner with your parents tonight?"

I started to cry as I told him the whole story. He let me get it all out – both tears and words – and then he said, "Screw them. You messed up. You apologized. You needed to be heard, too, and they couldn't do that. So screw them."

I took a big sip of my beer and thanked the Trappists for their dedication to fine ale before I said, "Screw them." And then cried a bit more.

Eventually, though, I ran out of tears and got around to telling Daniel what Woody and I had learned at the Harris farm today. "I can't really call it a farm, though," I said after I gave him the lowdown on the oil wells. "It's more an estate really with a farm décor theme. It was like something out of one of those HGTV shows where they do a farmhouse remodel on the 65,000-square-foot mansion by incorporating shiplap and lots of porches."

Daniel laughed, "You make fun, and yet we have watched exactly nineteen versions of that same show."

I smiled. "It just doesn't make any sense. I mean if everyone knows about the oil, why were Pickle and Bear talking about it like it was some great secret? And why wouldn't Miranda just come clean about the inheritance rather than acting like she had nothing to gain? Surely, even she knows that honesty in a murder investigation is your best bet?"

"Maybe she doesn't know?" Daniel said as he put the mug of delicious ale to his lips. "Maybe she doesn't know she's a millionaire now?"

5

I came to work on Tuesday morning feeling a little down. Over the years, I'd come to terms with who my parents were and that they weren't the parents who were going to show up for the big moments in my life with a bouquet of flowers and enthusiasm. But sometimes, especially when I knew I'd tried to avoid who they were instead of just dealing with it, I let my disappointment in them get to me.

But I had a business to run, and for yet another reason, I was grateful for this little shop, these people I worked with, and most of all for the books. Books had always been my refuge, a safe space where I could let my large, powerful emotions have free reign beside the characters on the pages. This morning, I arrived at the shop a few minutes after nine and grabbed Philip Pullman's *The Amber Spyglass* off the shelf, turned to what I thought was one of the most heartbreaking passages in literature, and let myself sob alongside Lyra.

By the time Marcus arrived, I was feeling better, all my emotions poured out and not repressed, and ready for the day. It didn't hurt that Marcus bounced through the door with Taco at his heels and said, "New book day, Ms. B" with the enthusiasm of Tigger.

"I see you brought reinforcements," I pointed at the lumbering form of Daniel's Basset Hound.

"I figured we could use his ability to sleep as the reverse psychology of motivation."

I laughed as Taco dropped onto his side, missing the dog bed on which Mayhem lay with everything but his tail.

Tuesday always was my favorite day in the bookshop – all those new titles to display, all those customers coming in with excitement for their favorite author's new book. I couldn't stay melancholy with all that to look forward to.

Marcus and I busied ourselves with helping customers and rearranging the new titles table at the front of the shop. Rocky supplied us with cups of her new dark roast from the local coffee roasters and lemon scones that were just the right balance of tart and sweet. Nothing like good books and baked goods.

Just as Marcus was about to take his lunch, Galen Gilbert came in with Mack, and we had a low and rather slow dog version of the running of the bulls among the bookshelves as Taco, Mayhem, and Mack played. Taco was a usual fixture at the shop now as it was far safer for everyone if he was here and not leaning against car jacks in Daniel's shop. Marcus took it as part of his duty as the renter in Daniel's apartment to pick up the pup each morning, and the two had become fast friends.

Now, he was corralling the three pooches to the bed in the front window before he went out the door with a wave.

Galen was, hands down, my favorite customer. He was, first and foremost, a mystery reader, but he also liked "expanding his horizons," as he put it and asked me often for recommendations. Last week, I'd put Edward Ball's *Slaves in the Family* into his hands when he said he wanted some history but nothing dry. Now, I was eager to hear what he thought.

"Well?" I asked as he leaned against the counter by the register. "Did you like it?"

He looked down at his hands and cleared his throat. "Not exactly, Harvey." Then he looked up through the top of his eyes and said, "I loved it. What a brilliant amount of work Ball did, and I loved how honest he was about his family's legacy as slave holders. Wow. I'll be thinking about that one for a long time."

"I thought you'd love it. It's so good. I wish more people knew about it."

Galen grinned and held up his phone. "They do now."

On the screen was an image of a person's shoulder just outside the front of my store with the sign clear as day, and I laughed. "I need to hire you as my PR manager, sir." He handed me the phone, and I read his glowing caption that had, in the first five minutes, 656 likes. "You are a master."

"I can only do my work with the support of worthy experts like you." He laughed and headed off to the mystery section.

I did a lap around the shop to tidy and say hello to the folks reading and browsing among the shelves, and when I circled back, Galen had returned to the register with his usual stack of titles. "You've read Lauren Elliot, I presume," he said as I began to ring up the books, sliding my twenty percent employee discount into the mix as a bit of gratitude for his publicity.

"Just this first one, so far. But I loved it." I slipped *Murder by the Book* into the tote Galen always brought with him and finished ringing up his other purchases. "Thank you, Galen. For everything."

"My pleasure, Harvey. Really. You've made my life better with your shop, and Mack loves coming here, too." We looked over to see Mayhem giving Mack a face bath with her tongue. "Plus, the free spa services are a delight as well."

I laughed and waved as he clipped a leash onto a lumbering Mack and headed out the door.

As usual, the day got busier as people took lunch breaks and coffee breaks and "book breaks," as the woman who ran the yarn shop down the street called her daily visit to the shop. Plus, a number of folks who stopped by told me they'd seen Galen's posts about the shop and finally decided to visit since they lived nearby. Every time I saw some young twenty-something come into the store and hold up Galen's Instagram feed to show me why they were here, I wondered if they knew who was behind that beautiful assortment of images and book recommendations. Galen used Mack as his profile pic, and I thought that was probably a thoughtful choice.

A BIT later in the day, I was straightening up the children's sections that had been beautifully pillaged by the after-school crowd when two men came in. The slimmer of the two was a white man, about sixty or so with a moustache that turned up at the ends, and the other was a balding black man with just the beginning of a potbelly. "Pickle and Bear!" I didn't mean to say their names – especially their nicknames – out loud, but clearly I had, because they both turned toward me as I prized myself up from the floor by the easy readers.

"You must be Harvey Beckett." Bear put out his hand. "We've been meaning to stop by and say hello. My wife simply raves about you and your shop."

For a split second I thought about playing dumb, but given that I'd just shouted their small-town nicknames across the store, I figured the jig was up and shook his hand saying, "You must be

Bear. I mean, is it okay if I call you Bear?" I sucked my breath in through my teeth.

"Unless you're my mother and prefer Berrington Rutherford Johnson." He laughed. "Everyone calls me Bear."

I smiled. "I don't know. Berrington Rutherford has a certain ring to it."

"My mother believed that names set up a person for life, giving them power and stature that supports them each day. She was thoroughly disgusted when the nickname Bear arrived as I started kindergarten and became notorious for giving 'bear hugs' to all the girls."

"A ladies' man from a young age, I see." I winked. "It appears your mother and mine shared that perspective. My given name is Anastasia Lovejoy."

Bear's eyes got wide. "That is quite the name."

"Indeed it is. You can see why I stuck with Harvey."

The other man put out his hand, and I shook it. "Pickle Herring, ma'am. I probably don't have to explain . . ."

I gave him a wink. "I think I got it." I swung my arm in an arc behind me. "What brings you into my fine establishment, gentlemen?"

"Can't two people just want to visit the newest shop in town?" Bear looked at me slyly.

"Of course they can, but if you don't mind me saying, I do believe you are the first pair of men – who weren't a couple – who have come into the shop. Unless there's something you haven't revealed to the town yet."

Both men leaned back and laughed. "You are not the first person to suggest this possibility, Harvey, but no, just friends here," Pickle said.

"To be truthful, we heard that you were curious about some treasure over at Huckabee Harris's house," Bear said with a small smile.

I shouldn't have been surprised. There were *no* secrets in St. Marin's, but still, I thought we'd been pretty discrete, at least about how Bear and Pickle were connected to our visit yesterday. I sighed. "You found me out. Word travels fast around here." I pointed to the café. "Buy you a cup of coffee?"

The men looked at each other and shrugged. We took a table by the window, and given that the gossip train had already run its way right back to me again, I figured our public conversation would either be the source of great speculation or silence the chatter.

As I went up to the counter to get our coffee, Rocky said, "Pickle and Bear are notorious pranksters, Harvey. Even worse than the sheriff. I'll put on these lids to keep your coffee from being laced with salt or something." I brought three cups from a fresh pot of that delicious dark roast back to the table and set them down before going back for a small carton of half and half and a sugar jar.

"Let's lay it all out there. Who told you I was, er, investigating?"

Pickle looked at Bear and then over at me before saying, "Mum's the word. We don't reveal our sources." He gave me a wink. "Besides, it doesn't really matter. Everyone at breakfast heard the story."

"So I'm the talk of the town, huh?" I joked.

"Have been for about a month now, my lady," Bear said.

I blushed. "Well, I hope the rumors are making me out to be amazing."

"How could they not?" Bear laughed and took a sip of his coffee.

"So you two want to get into the oil business." I said with a smile as I took my first sip.

"Oil? What are you talking about, woman?" Pickle said as he leaned forward in his chair. "We aren't interested in any oil."

I almost spit out my coffee, but managed to swallow it first. "You're not interested in the oil at Harris's place."

Another look between them. Another shrug. "Whatever gave you that idea?"

I tried to put together the train of thought that had made that seem so obvious, but as I did, I realized I'd jumped a lot of tracks to get to that particular station. My turn to shrug. "It seemed like buried treasure, I guess."

"You know Miranda gets all that, right? And we've got no problem with that. She's got enough problems, and maybe that'll be a way for her to solve some of them."

I put up a little mental note to come back to Miranda's problems, but I didn't want to lose the treasure track again. I suddenly had an idea, and I tried not to snicker when it came to mind. "You're looking for Confederate gold."

Without a second's pause, Bear shouted, "Darn tootin' we are, young lady! Even have a map."

Pickle snapped, "Bear!"

I looked from man to man, trying to get a read on these two fellows who appeared far too smart to buy into that fool's legend. The scowl Pickle was giving Bear after he mentioned that map looked pretty serious. "Don't worry, fellas, I won't be horning in on your treasure hunt. But you do know that most of those rumors," I wanted to say *all of those rumors*, but didn't like to dash people's hopes, "aren't true, right?"

Bear looked at me like I was pointing out the earth was flat and said, "Of course we know that. We're not just some country bumpkins who fell off the turnip truck."

I smiled at the lovely mix of metaphors.

Pickled leaned over the table. "But this one is true. Huckabee's grandmother herself told me about it."

"His grandmother? Really?" I figured I might as well get their full story. If nothing else, my friends would love to hear all about it.

"Yep. On her death bed. She leaned over and said, 'By the willow, Pickle. By the willow.'" He sat back firmly in his seat like those seven words settled it.

I nodded solemnly, even as I puzzled over why Pickle was at the deathbed of someone else's grandmother. "So the treasure is by the willow then?"

Bear rolled his eyes. "Pay attention. No, that's where the map was."

"Oh, I see," I said with gravitas. "Can I see the map?"

Bear looked at Pickle, and Pickle gave a slight nod. A smartphone was laid in front of me, and I saw a photo of what looked like a drawing done by a third grader – or by me. I was not the finest artist and still employed the farmhouse with a long lane against a mountain backdrop with a sun in the corner technique that this artist also used.

The "map" showed a building with four windows equally placed on the front façade and surrounding a door. A couple of waving lines that were roughly parallel ran up to that door, and in the background, some arcs that overlapped formed what I assumed were mountains. On one of the mountains, a thin line disappeared at the peak, and of course, there was a sun drawn in the upper right-hand corner.

Pickle's thick pointer finger drew my attention to the squiggle on the mountain. "You see that? That's a road."

"Yep," Bear added. "We've studied the outlines of these hills, and we know just where they are."

"Let me guess. On the Harris property?"

"This girl's smart, Pickle." Bear grinned at his friend.

"Sure is, but not smart enough to know when she's been played," Pickle said matter-of-factly.

Both men turned and looked at me, and I just stared at them. "What?" I finally spit out.

Their roars of laughter echoed through the store and still I stared, trying to figure out why they were laughing when I'd just been told the most ridiculous tale of treasure hunting. And that's when it hit me, and I felt a blush run all the way from my chest to my scalp. "You are pulling my leg."

Bear wheezed out, "Did anyone ever tell you *gullible* isn't in the dictionary?"

That tired joke sent the two of them into another fit of laughter.

I watched these two men roll in their chairs, and while my pride was a little dinged up, I found myself laughing, too. Soon all three of us were wiping tears from our eyes and trying to get our breath.

"You got me, fellows. You got me good."

Pickle took a pair of tortoiseshell glasses in the latest style out of his pocket and put them on his nose before smoothing back his hair into a very business-like style just as Bear stood up, tucked in his shirt, and slid a sports jacket on over his button-down. Clearly these two had planned this . . . and I suddenly had a suspicion. "Sheriff Mason put you up to this, didn't he?"

"I cannot tell a lie," Bear said with his hand over his heart. "So I'm not going to say anything at all.

And speak of the devil, in came our esteemed sheriff himself. He took one look at the three of us and bent over double with amusement. "You got her, didn't you?" he said between bursts of laughter.

"Hook, line, and Confederate gold sinker," Pickle said.

"Woody told you we went to the Harris place," I said to the sheriff as I got up from the table. "Didn't he?"

"Serves you right for snooping around about a murder." He was still laughing, but I could also hear the reminder in his words.

"You're right, I guess. But I mean, I found the body. I have a vested—"

"Stop right there, Harvey." The sheriff wasn't laughing anymore. "I know you want to know what happened. We all do. But you can't be digging into police matters. It's not wise, and it might be dangerous."

I sighed. I knew he was right, and a small part of me wanted to heed his caution. But I already knew I wouldn't.

The sheriff's radio squawked, and he put it to his ear as he turned down the volume. "Gotta go, folks. Rocky, you got all that, right?"

I looked over at my friend and saw her grin. "What's he talking about, Rocky?"

"Already emailed the video to you, Sheriff."

"Good woman," he said as he went out the door.

"Rocky Chevalier, you were in on this?"

She shrugged. "If you could have seen your face . . ."

I gave her my strongest fake glare, then smiled and sat back down.

"You do know that the two of you owe me now, right?"

Bear nodded as he took a napkin and scribbled on it. "Consider this our IOU."

"Is that what this says?" I stared down at the napkin at what looked like a toddler's first drawing.

Bear grinned. "I do have another favor to ask, though." I gave him a skeptical look as he continued. "Henry sent over a list of books that I'm supposed to bring her when I leave. I have explicit instructions to ask you to order them if you don't have them in stock." He handed me a sheet of notebook paper with about twenty titles on it.

"Wow. She's quite the reader." I gave the list a scan. "I think we have most of these, but it'll take me a while to pull them. Why don't I bring them to Henry later this afternoon?"

"Well, that's what I call service . . ." Bear squinted, "But I suspect that this generosity may come with a price tag. How may we help?"

"You mentioned that Miranda Harris-Lewis had problems. I take it that this wasn't just part of your ruse."

Pickle looked at me askance. "You haven't heard?" When I shook my head, he said, "Oh. Her husband is, well, what we might call in my line of work, a repeat offender."

"He's got a criminal record?"

Bear almost shouted, "No, and that's the problem. That woman has more bruises and bumps to the head than any person I've ever known, and I've been an ER doctor for three decades."

"He beats her?" I whispered, imagining the perfectly put-together woman who was here the day before.

"No doubt about it in anyone's mind, but she won't press charges or leave him. She's too scared," Pickle said quietly. "And honestly, she has reason to be. Rafe Lewis is a dangerous man."

"Oh, that's terrible." I sighed. "I had a friend back in California who was in a similar situation. It took her years to leave, but when she did, she never looked back."

"May it be so for that poor woman." Bear's voice was somber.

"That's the reason for the falling out with her dad, I imagine. I mean neither of them seems like the most warm and fuzzy of personalities, but it takes a special kind of damage to make a child give up on a parent."

"I expect so," Pickle said as he stood. "Now, I need to get back to the office. I've got depositions starting in an hour."

Bear rose on the other side of me. "And my shift starts at the hospital in thirty minutes. Thank you for a great laugh, Harvey. That's one of our finest pieces of work."

I smiled and walked with them to the door. They had already swung it open when I realized something. "Guys, wait? What did my mother overhear you talking about then? What's the treasure?"

"Oil, my dear. Black gold," Pickle said.

Bear nodded. "We're buying the mineral rights to the land from Miranda. Giving her a great return with the hopes she can put it to good use."

My throat got a little tight. "That seems like an incredibly kind thing to do, gentlemen."

"We try, my lady, we try," Bear said as he slid a flat top hat on his head and walked out the door with his friend.

THAT NIGHT, everyone gathered at my house for pizza night. Lucas and Cate brought homemade dough, Elle brought a salad fresh from her garden, Mart and I contributed the cheese, meat and sauce, and Daniel and Marcus got the beverages. I'd suggested the idea of a get-together – with food, always with food – when I'd texted everyone to say I had to catch them up on things, and everyone was game, except Rocky who had to study for her exams. I'd offered to quiz her over pizza, but she wisely pointed out that wine and nineteenth century British literature probably weren't a good combo.

While we stretched the dough, spread the sauce, and chose our toppings, I told the tale of Pickle and Bear's prank. Mart was a little defensive on my behalf – "Oh, Harvey, that must have been so embarrassing."

I laughed. "It was, but then it wouldn't have been a good joke if it wasn't, right? Besides, unless Rocky puts the video on YouTube, I feel pretty safe knowing it'll just be St. Marin's folks who hear about it."

"Oh no. You don't think she'd put that up do you?" Mart looked genuinely alarmed.

I put an arm around her shoulders. "You are so sweet. No, she would never do that. Don't worry." Mart had been working nonstop for two days and had raced home after her last meeting for dinner. She was exhausted, and like me, when she was tired, her emotions got bigger and came right to the surface. "Besides, if it did go live, people would just laugh."

"Or go hunting for that Confederate gold because their attention spans didn't last through the punchline," Cate said as she spread a glorious amount of mozzarella on her pizza.

We got the pizza onto trays and into the oven and then all took our beverages to the living room to chat. "But I haven't told you the really interesting part yet." I felt a little bad for talking about Miranda's abuse this way, but I knew my friends would be more concerned than lurid in their listening. And I really wanted their thoughts on whether Rafe Lewis could have killed Miranda's dad.

I shared what Pickle and Bear had told me, and no one but Mart was surprised. Even Daniel, who was notoriously out of the loop about town tales, nodded when I shared what I'd learned. "You knew?" I asked him when I was done.

"Of course I knew. Everyone in town knows."

"But you didn't think to tell me?"

He shrugged. "I try not to gossip, Harvey. I didn't know how it would be relevant, and to be truthful, the abuse has been going on so long that I kind of forgot about it." He winced. "I know that sounds awful."

"No, I know what you mean," Lucas added. "I think everyone in town has tried to help her. Cate here even offered to let her and the girls live with us. But she's never accepted help. In fact, she gets defensive and sort of mean when someone offers. Eventually, everyone stopped asking."

"She's terrified. It's not rational, but it seems like she thinks if she accepts help, then Rafe will find out, and it'll get worse for her. She may well be right." Cate's voice was tender.

"Are the girls okay?" I asked. "I mean, child protective services?"

Marcus shook his head violently. "That would only make things worse. I don't think the girls are getting hurt. At least, when I see them, they're quiet and almost too obedient, but I've never seen sign of a physical injury."

Cate nodded. "I agree. That doesn't mean they aren't being traumatized of course, poor things, but Marcus is right. If we call CPS and they come and do a wellness check and don't find cause to remove the girls, then they could be Rafe's next victims."

I curled my legs up under me and took a big swig of my chardonnay. "I guess, too, then Miranda would get it even worse." I put my head against Daniel's shoulder.

Mart sniffled. "So there's nothing we can do?"

We all sat quietly for a few moments until the oven timer went off and startled us all.

"Well, time to eat." Lucas stood and helped Cate up from the floor. It felt a little callous to just move on after a conversation like that, but we had other business to attend to . . . namely trying to figure out if Miranda killed her father as her escape.

"So she could have done it, I guess," Elle said between bites, "but she was going to inherit all that wealth anyway, right? Plus, don't we think her dad would have given her anything she asked for?"

I shook my head slowly. "I'm finding it hard to imagine Huckabee Harris as a doting father," an image of my dad standing at the cash register in the shop came to mind, "but I suspect every father is protective of his baby girl."

"Exactly. But maybe Huckabee put conditions on his generosity. Maybe he said Miranda had to leave Rafe, and she just wouldn't – or couldn't – do that." Cate's voice was strident. "Terror can make a person very irrational."

I peeled the cheese off my slice of pizza and ate it before saying, "Okay, so maybe she's still a possible suspect. But it sounds like we need to consider other options, too."

"Like Rafe," Daniel said. "I mean if Huckabee was trying to get Miranda to leave him . . ."

"That's a good point," Marcus said. "Maybe he took care of the one escape route Miranda had.

I put my pizza down and pulled my sweater tighter around me. "This guy. I hope I don't meet him in a dark alley."

Cate looked at me intently, "I'd suggest trying not to meet him at all. He's pretty scary."

Mart nodded then said. "But something is bothering me. It's the oil. I mean, I don't know how oil wells work, but no one is living out there now. Couldn't someone just be stealing the oil?"

"Well, Homer is out there. I expect he's keeping an eye on things."

From the blank expressions on most of the faces in the room, I realized that I hadn't yet mentioned Homer. "Ah, he's the caretaker. The farm manager, I think he said his title was. Nice guy. Friend of Woody's."

Mart nodded. "So the oil is safe, and that means whoever killed Huckabee still doesn't have access to the oil." Her eyes got very wide. "Oh no, what if Homer is in danger?"

She had a point, but I'd seen him packing a pretty big pistol on his hip. I figured he could handle himself, and my friends agreed when I told them about the gun.

We tossed around theories about who could have killed Huckabee – an angry shop owner who had been at the brunt of his forceful attitude, a disgruntled employee, etc. – but when we our conversation devolved into a *Criminal Minds*-like theory on serial killers, Daniel suggested that perhaps our conversation had gone as far as it could . . . and also that maybe we should all watch a little less TV.

As Mart, Daniel, and I cleaned up, my mind kept returning to Miranda and to the girls. Suddenly, I knew what I had to do. I also knew my friends would not approve so I kept my mouth shut and loaded the dishwasher.

I walked Daniel and Marcus to the door. Marcus said goodnight and went on ahead to wait for Daniel in his truck.

"Thank you for being here," I said as I looked up into his face.

"Always, Harvey. Always." He leaned down and gave me a tender kiss and then led Taco down the walk. I closed the door and leaned against it, feeling peaceful. That man always made me feel peaceful.

But then Mart rounded the corner, stood in front of me with her hands on her hips, and said, "You have that look, Harvey."

"Look? What look?" I asked, not meeting her eyes.

"The one where your jaw tightens just a bit, and your brow furrows. The look that says you have a plan."

Gracious, there were downsides to having a best friend. I poured us another glass of wine and told Mart what I thought I'd do the next day. She didn't like it, but "I'm in," she said. "You need a wing woman for this kind of venture."

There were upsides to having a best friend, too.

$\mathcal{T}$he next morning, we stopped at the shop and saw that Marcus had things well in hand before we headed to Miranda's house. I'd checked in with Cate who had told me what car Rafe drove – a black Audi A8 with dark tinted windows. I had no idea what that looked like, so I texted Daniel, who sent me a picture. Pretty much what I'd imagined a man like him might drive – super expensive (like $85,000 expensive), super sleek, super pretentious.

She also said that he worked at an accounting firm over in Annapolis so would likely be gone most of the day. "But be careful, Harvey. We've all seen the movie where the husband comes home early and finds the person snooping. Don't get caught."

The fact that I hadn't told her what I was doing was not lost on me. I clearly was not as sneaky as I thought I was with my casual fact-finding queries.

The Harris-Lewis's lived in a gated community just south of St. Marin's. It had only taken a quick GIS search to find their address.

I'd driven past the neighborhood a few times on my trips up and down Route 13 when I'd first moved here, and every time I was shocked at the size of these homes. "Why would anyone want that much square footage inside their house when they can practically look in the windows of their neighbor's houses AND still have to drive to go do anything?" I'd asked that question so many times that Mart had finally stopped trying to answer me.

Now, she and I sat at the gate flummoxed by how to get in. There was no gatehouse, so we couldn't do the "surprise visit to our sister" ruse we'd come up with. The giant metal gate made ramming out of the question. (Also, Mart was disinclined to damage her Prius.) Finally, we settled for the old "fake that we've lost our key fob" ploy by parking at the gate and then waiting until a car approached so we could rummage around looking for it.

For the record, people in the South are fairly trusting folks. We want to believe people mean well. So I wasn't surprised at all when the first car that approached from the inside of the gate – a mini-van simply stuffed with car seats – stopped. A woman who looked to be about thirty and perfect – immaculate hair, pristine make-up, a tiny scarf tied around her neck – leaned out the driver's side window and said, "You okay?"

In the back seats of the van, I could see small heads bobbing around, but there was no sound. Only on closer inspection did I notice that they each had a screen and headphones. I wanted to give her a hug and praise her for her wisdom. With that many kids – heck, even with one kid – I could totally see how screens had become ubiquitous with children.

Mart brushed her hair up off her forehead. "Oh yeah, we're fine. I mean, mostly. I can't find my keychain thingy to get us in. I thought I'd left it in the cup holder, but my toddler climbs around in here like it's his jungle gym, and now, well . . ."

Smart move to play the kid card, except of course for the lack of the car seat in the back. I hoped this wizard Mom wouldn't notice.

"Oh I know what you mean. My littlest ate one once. Here, use mine." She passed her keychain out of the window, and I marveled yet again at cars that didn't need keys in their ignitions.

Mart waved the entire keychain in front of the small gray box by the gate, and presto, it opened right up. She handed the keys back and said, "Thank you so much."

"No problem." Super Mom started to put up the window but then lowered it again. "Oh, and check the drawers in the refrigerator. It's amazing what I've found there."

I laughed, and Mart gave her a thumbs up. We drove through the gate just as it started to swing shut again, and I thought about how I'd like to be friends with that woman.

My attention was quickly drawn back to the task at hand when we pulled up in front of a beautiful house with a gorgeous stone façade. The three-car garage didn't even seem big against the size of this massive specimen of home life, and I found myself slightly envious . . . until I saw the exact same house three doors down and then three doors after that. I just wasn't a fan of cookie-cutter houses, even if they were beautiful. I expected Miranda Harris-Lewis wouldn't be a fan of our little craftsman bungalow either. I figured that was fair.

I snuck up to the garage and was grateful they had splurged on the doors with panes of glass in them. As soon as I looked in, I realized they splurged on a lot – those miniature Jeeps, two of them for the girls; bicycles that looked like they cost more than my entire wardrobe; and a very swanky and shiny SUV. But no Audi A8. We were good to go.

I gave Mart the very subtle signal of a big "come on" wave, and we headed toward the front door. I wasn't interested in pulling one over on Miranda. I figured the performance this jerk had put on to get her to marry him was enough duping for one lifetime. Instead, we were going in honest with an offer to help.

My hope was that as the new people in town she might realize we don't know the backstory but also that the reality of her situation was so obvious that even we knew. For whatever reason, I was often the person who others chose to talk to. Maybe it's because I loved stories so much that even getting to listen to people talk about their lives was exciting to me. Or maybe I just had one of *those* faces. For whatever reason, I often knew people's hardest moments and deepest shames. I hoped my listening gift would work now because I wanted to figure out who killed Huckabee Harris. But even more, I really wanted to help Miranda.

We rang the bell, and I heard a tinkling sound like wind chimes inside. A few minutes later, the sound of little feet came through the door and then the door opened to Maisy and Daisy in pink, unicorn PJs. Their faces were covered in chocolate, and it looked like a brush hadn't been put their hair in days. This was not a good sign.

"Hi girls. I don't know if you remember me, but I'm Harvey Beckett from—"

"Oh we remember," Daisy or Maisy said. There had to be a trick for keeping them straight, I just knew it. "From the bookstore."

"Well, okay, good. Actually, we're here to see your mom. Is she available?"

They looked at each other and then up at us. "She's sick. She'll be better this afternoon before Daddy comes home."

I looked at Mart and held back a gasp. "Girls, is she okay? Does she need help?"

They shrugged, but something about their expressions – a
mixture of concern and helplessness – made me think the actual
answer was yes.

Mart knelt down. "I'm Mart. Harvey's best friend. Do you think
you could do us a favor and go tell your mom we're here and
that we'd like to see her, that we can come to her if she wants?"

They nodded and then ran up the wide staircase behind them.

"Mart, this is terrible. Why aren't those girls in school? What is
going on?"

My friend looked like she was going to cry, and I felt pretty close
myself. But we kept it together and waited.

A few minutes later, one of the girls came to the top of the stairs
and said, "Mommy says you can come in. But only for a few
minutes."

I sighed, stepped inside, and closed the door. So much for
keeping an eye out for Rafe.

We climbed to the top of the stairs and then followed Maisy or
Daisy to a room at the end of the hall where the other sister was
waiting. They swung the door open and stepped aside.

Inside, I saw the most beautiful bedroom and the most forlorn
person I'd ever seen. Miranda was in bed, and she looked like
she'd been through three rounds with a prize fighter. Both eyes
were black, her jaw was swollen, and on the tips of her arms, I
could see hand prints.

I took a deep breath, glanced at Mart, and then climbed into bed
next to Miranda. Mart took the girls downstairs while asking
about their favorite TV shows, and I slid until my shoulder
rested against Miranda's. Then, she dropped her head to my
shoulder and began to sob.

I put my arm around her carefully and let her cry. After a few minutes, she started to settle, and eventually, she sat up and looked at me. "I'm so sorry. I don't know what came over me."

"It's okay. I have that effect on people." I gave her a small smile.

"You make them cry?" She smiled back.

"Far too often, I'm afraid." I turned to face her. "Miranda, are you okay? I mean really?"

Tears pooled in her eyes again, and she shook her head. "But I guess you can see that, can't you?"

I looked at her bruised arms and battered face and nodded. "I can. And you don't deserve this, Miranda."

She started to say something while shaking her head, but I put up my hand with the palm toward her.

"Nope, there's nothing, not a thing in the world you could have done or said that made you deserve this. You need to believe that." I looked at her until her eyes met mine.

"I know." She sighed. "I mean part of me knows, but the other part – the part that loves him – wants to believe that I'm the problem." Her eyes started to well up again. "Because if he's the problem, then I love a monster."

I had never thought about domestic abuse that way, that it meant that you had to believe a horrible thing about someone you loved. I was no stranger to being treated terribly by men, but I had been fortunate to not have been a victim of actual abuse.

I took her hands in mine. "I can't even imagine how hard this is. I'm so sorry."

She pulled her eyes up from the bedspread and looked at me again. "Thank you."

I squeezed her fingers.

"No really." She grabbed my hands tightly. "A lot of people have offered to help me by giving us a place to stay or cash. But no one has ever come to my house before. Not a single person."

I must have looked puzzled because she continued, "The gate keeps people out, which is what Rafe wants of course. He likes our 'privacy,' he says." I could hear what I hoped was a good, hard edge coming into her voice now. "But people are also scared of him . . . or maybe they're scared of what he'll do to me if he finds out they're here." She sat bolt upright then. "Oh no, the camera."

Her alarm startled me. "What camera?"

"The doorbell camera. He'll know you've been here. You have to leave. *Now!*" She jumped up from the bed, pulling me with her.

"Wait, Miranda? What's going on?"

"He gets an alert anytime that doorbell camera is triggered. I'm not allowed to have visitors. Please, you have to go. It's not safe."

I rushed into the hall after her while I tried to think of what was worse, Rafe coming home to find us here or Rafe coming home to find us already gone. Neither sounded great, but I figured we might be able to actually protect Miranda if we were here.

The two of us ran down the stairs into the living room where Mart and the girls were watching TV. "Maisy and Daisy, Daddy will be home any minute."

Those two little girls blanched and jumped to their feet, putting dolls into houses and toys into boxes with a speed that I could never have matched.

"They have a doorbell cam," I told Mart.

"He will lose it if the house is a mess," Miranda said as she ran her hand through her hair. "Oh my god. I have to fix myself up."

Mart grabbed the woman's hand and dragged her upstairs. "I'll help. No time for a shower, but we can work with your hair, and I've got the make-up skills of a Broadway artist."

Miranda in good hands, I knelt down and said to Maisy and Daisy. "What else?"

They looked and each other and shouted, "The kitchen."

I jogged after them into the largest, most ornate kitchen I'd ever seen. It looked immaculate, but the girls must have seen it in a way I did not because they went right to work wiping counters and putting away dishes. I finally shouted, "How can I help?"

Maisy/Daisy said, "Light the candle there. And wipe all the fingerprints off the fridge." She tossed me a book of matches and a rag, and I did as I was told.

The girls did one quick look around the room and nodded, and then I said, "Do you need to be dressed?"

They shot up the stairs quick as lightning, and I sat on the bottom stair, trying to think. We had to have a reason for why we were there, a reason that wouldn't make Rafe mad and would also justify our visit.

I was at the edges of an idea when I heard the garage door open and four sets of feet thunder down the steps toward me. Miranda looked perfect, and the girls were adorable in leggings and sweaters with sparkly headbands over their mostly brushed hair. I pushed a stray lock under Daisy/Maisy's headband as she passed.

I pointed toward what looked to be a formal sitting room and said, "In there." Then, I grabbed my purse where I'd set it by the front door and took out the gifts I'd brought for Maisy and Daisy. We had all just dropped into our seats, still breathing heavily, when a very thin white man in a deep charcoal suit and one silver earring barreled into the room.

"What is going on here?" he boomed.

I stood up and put on the biggest smile I could muster before extending my hand to this man. I hoped he couldn't see it shaking. "Mr. Lewis," I was banking on the idea that he hadn't taken Miranda's maiden name when they'd married, "I'm Harvey Beckett. I run the new bookstore in town. My clerk and I just stopped by to tell your family that we'd like to feature your daughters in a new ad campaign for the store. They are such delightful little girls, and we think they'd make great models to encourage other children to read."

Miranda looked positively terrified when I glanced at her, but she was smiling. The girls had a similar expression.

I looked back at Rafe and shot out a prayer to whoever was listening. *Please let him believe me.* Rafe still looked angry, but somehow, I could tell the suspicion had fallen away. He bought it.

"Your wife here kindly invited us in to explain so that she could get all the details to talk with you about them later." I picked up the two Magic Tree House books I'd set on the coffee table. "Maisy and Daisy were in last week when Mrs. Lewis was running errands in town, and they mentioned they loved these books. So I brought a couple for them." I prayed I hadn't just caused more trouble by mentioning that Miranda had been in town, but he didn't seem to be surprised, so I hoped I was okay.

Mart stood, "Anyway, we were just going. Thank you for your time, Mrs. Lewis." She shook Miranda's hand.

I stepped to Miranda and shook her hand, too, slipping my business card with my cell number into her fingers. "When you guys have had time to discuss the details, please give me a call. No pressure and no expectations from us. Whatever you decide is just fine." I backed away while I tried to assure Miranda with my expression that we weren't abandoning her, just trying to keep her safe.

Mart offered her hand to Rafe as she walked past, and he shook it before taking mine again. "Thank you, ladies. We don't get many guests, but I appreciate your visit. We'll talk it over and get back to you."

He walked us to the door while Miranda and the girls stayed behind. I hated leaving them, but I knew that pushing this situation was not wise . . . for any of us.

Mart and I walked silently back to the car and got in. She carefully pulled out as I tried to contain the sobs that were threatening to explode. I had no doubt that man was watching us from the window, and I didn't want to give him any reason to doubt our story.

As we turned the corner, Mart gasped, and I doubled over. "Mart?! What do we do?"

"I don't know yet, Harvey. But something. We do something."

On the way back to the store, I texted Sheriff Mason to ask him to come by. I had to report what I saw and ask his wisdom. I knew he wouldn't do anything to put Miranda in harm's way, and I really, really needed his advice. She could be permanently hurt if that kind of battery continued, and while I hadn't seen any signs of physical assault against the girls, there was no way that kind of fear made for a safe living environment.

When we walked in, Rocky pointed to a table she'd set up with shortbread, a thermos of coffee, and three chairs. "Cate texted me," she said quietly.

I checked in with Marcus, who was just fine, and dropped into the chair next to Mart. We sat in silence and took tiny nibbles from the cookies. I had put an extra dose of cream and sugar in my coffee. I needed fortification.

By the time Sheriff Mason arrived, my nerves were less jangled, and I could take a deep breath again. Now, though, I was furious, so mad that I didn't even let the sheriff sit down before I said, "You need to arrest Rafe Lewis. Today. He's an abuser, and he's beating his wife."

"You went to see her, didn't you?" The sheriff's voice sounded both sad and frustrated.

"We did." Mart was angry, too, but her voice was also very quiet. "We put her in danger, didn't we?"

Sheriff Mason sat down. "You did. But I know that wasn't your intention. Rafe Lewis is a very violent man, and we have known for a long time that he was hitting Miranda. But she's never pressed charges. The two times I've seen her in the hospital when she's had broken bones so severe that Bear was legally obligated to report suspected domestic violence, she's refused. We have tried, but unless we see him hitting her or she makes an official statement, I can do absolutely nothing."

I wanted to cry again. "I hear you, Sheriff. And I believe you, but we saw what he had done to her."

"What did you see, Harvey? Tell me. I do want to hear." He was looking at me then, and I could see how angry and frustrated he was.

"Two black eyes. Major bruises on her upper arms. A swollen jaw. And that doesn't include what was underneath her clothes." Mart sat forward. "I saw that. Her body is one big bruise, and I think she has a few broken ribs. It's awful."

The sheriff shook his head. "Did he seem to suspect why you were there?"

"I don't think so," Mart said. "Harvey came up with a really plausible and innocuous reason for our visit."

I told Sheriff Tucker about our forthcoming media campaign where we hoped to featured Maisy and Daisy as our models. "He seemed to believe me."

"He probably would. He's a narcissist. His family is, as he sees it, an accessory to him. You were smart to flatter him by praising the girls. But be careful. No more visits. He's a suspicious SOB. Don't press your luck."

I nodded. "We won't. The way those girls reacted when they heard their father was coming home. It was bone-chilling. I don't want to put them in any more danger." Then I put my head down on my folded arms. "I'm so sorry. That was stupid."

The sheriff tousled the hair on the back of my head. "Stupid, but loving. I'll send an unmarked patrol car by a few times for the next couple of days. I don't know that it'll do any good, but maybe Miranda will see them and know that help is just outside."

"Thank you, Sheriff."

He headed toward the door but turned back long enough to say, "If you get the go ahead from him for the ad campaign, you know you have to do it, right?"

"I do. Fortunately, my good idea for that situation is probably also a good idea for the shop." How I'd pay for photographers and ad space I had no idea, but I was committed now. No way was I going to put the Harris-Lewis women in danger by flaking now.

MART STAYED at the store for the rest of the day to help Marcus, or so she said. But I figured she didn't want to be alone at home, and I didn't blame her. Our visit earlier had scared the life out of me, and I wanted the comfort of books, coffee, and good friends. We had our usual spattering of customers throughout the day, and when closing time came, all I wanted was a bowl of cereal, a hot bath, and some mindless TV – maybe *The Great British Baking Show* was on.

I had just gotten through two of the three parts of my evening plan when my phone rang. It was Sheriff Tucker. "Can I come by, Harvey?"

I looked down at my fluffy cow-print PJs and giant "Got Books?" T-shirt and shrugged. "Sure. I'll have hot cocoa ready." So much for learning how to make a cream cake using Mary Berry's recipe.

The sheriff looked harried when he came and fairly gulped the nearly boiling cup of hot cocoa when I offered it to him. "Whoa, slow down. You'll burn your throat away."

"Oh, yeah, sorry. I needed a jolt. It's been quite an evening." He pointed to the couch. "Mind if I sit?"

"Of course. You okay?"

"Yeah," he let out a hard breath. "Rafe Lewis was killed this afternoon."

"What?!" I almost shouted. "Mart, you need to hear this." She had taken her turn in the bath, but I knew she wouldn't want to miss the details and I didn't want to make the sheriff repeat himself. He looked exhausted.

While we waited for Mart to dry and dress, I got Mason another cup of cocoa and urged him to sip this one.

Mart sat down next to me. "What's up?"

"Rafe is dead," I said.

"He's what?"

"Murdered, actually. Run over by a car." The sheriff's voice was very quiet.

"Oh my gracious," I said. "And you're sure it wasn't an accident."

"I won't go into the details, but trust me when I say that there's plenty of evidence that it was intentional."

I let out a hard sigh. "Do you know who killed him?"

"Not yet . . . and Harvey, this really is not somewhere you should be snooping, okay?"

I gave him a look through the tops of my eyes. "I hear you. But any particular reason you're shooing me away this time?"

"You mean besides the fact that you're not a police officer?"

I shrugged. "Yeah, besides that."

"Because we suspect Miranda Harris-Lewis killed him.

7

To say the rest of that evening was restless would be akin to comparing Maryland's affection for Old Bay to my slight preference for walnut-honey cream cheese over berry cream cheese. In other words, there was no comparison.

I barely slept, and from the look of Mart the next morning, the same was true for her. We both could have played extras in a zombie film and wouldn't have needed to visit the make-up trailer.

I arrived at the store a bit before ten and was pleased to see that Marcus had already arrived for his shift and gone through the opening procedures. I had never been as glad as I was at that moment to have hired him.

Rocky was off that day for her classes, so Mart was covering the café . . . and I hoped she didn't scald herself with hot coffee. Sleep deprivation does not make for great coordination. Still, I was glad she was there again. We needed each other after the encounter with Rafe the day before and now this news about Miranda.

I had spent most of the night thinking about what the sheriff said, and while I really hoped that Miranda hadn't killed her husband, I couldn't say that I wouldn't understand. That man was awful, and he'd made her life and the life of her children miserable and terrifying. If she hadn't seen another way out, I could completely see how murder might have felt like her only option.

But somehow, I didn't believe it. She had seemed hopeful when we talked yesterday, and even though she'd looked absolutely terrified when we left, she hadn't tried to play off our ruse with a direct refusal. That made me think maybe she had wanted to use our ploy as a way of getting help. Maybe even getting out.

Still, she clearly had the most motive, and I could see why the sheriff suspected her. He'd said they were going to bring her in for questioning this morning and that I shouldn't contact her – even to check in – since that might tip her off. "For her sake, Harvey, we need this to be by the book. I only told you about our suspicions because of what happened earlier today. It was courtesy, but not permission."

I hadn't called, although I'd really wanted to. But I knew the sheriff was right. She had to react honestly in order for them to get this straight. So I waited.

FORTUNATELY, we were busy with our new children's story time for most of the morning. Each week, we'd had more and more preschoolers come with their parents, and I was loving the way they reacted to Marcus as he read to them from some of his favorite children's books. This week, he had chosen *Miss Rumphius* by Barbara Cooney, and as he read the story of a woman finding herself by planting flowers everywhere she went, his voice got wispy and magical. I, like the children at his feet, was swept away with the story. So swept away, in fact, that I didn't even see Sheriff Mason come in.

When story time ended, he was standing by the psychology bookshelf just outside the children's section, and he looked relaxed. I was hoping this wasn't just Marcus's gift for reading aloud or the beauty of the story. Maybe it also indicated that Miranda hadn't been arrested.

I sauntered over, trying to keep the buoyant feeling I had from the story, and said, "Oh, please, oh please, have good news."

He turned and smiled. "It wasn't her."

"Oh wow. Really. Okay, this is good news." I did a little spin and turned back to face Mason. "I mean, I know you still have to solve the case, but this is good news, right?"

"Yes, it's good news." His smile got bigger.

"So, how did you know?"

The smile faded quickly. "Harvey, you know I'm not going to tell you all the details. Let's just say that it was clear from the way she talked about driving that she was not capable of the, um, focus necessary to commit this murder."

I had no idea what that meant, and sometime later, I'd work a little harder to get the details. But now? Now I was just really happy.

The sheriff patted my shoulder. "I knew you'd want to know." He put on his hat and left.

I rushed over to the café to tell Mart the good news, and we did one of those jumpy, happy things that women always do on movies and that felt entirely unnatural, but also fitting.

"Oh, that's amazing," Mart said as she looked me hard in the eye. "But Harvey, this does not mean you can go sleuthing to find out who the killer is. You know that, right?"

I rolled my eyes. "Of course, I know that I'm not a trained investigator." I really, really wanted my dodge to go unnoticed but was not surprised when Mart gave my shoulders a little shake.

"That's not what I meant and you know it, Harvey Beckett. No snooping. No casual questioning. No studying of car bumpers. Nothing. You hear me?"

Her grip on my shoulders was firm, but I managed to duck and spin out. "I won't do anything dangerous. You know that."

"No, Harvey. No, I don't. Danger seems to find you because you are too darn curious."

But I was already walking away, a smile tossed over my shoulder, to help two men in the spirituality and religion section. I knew just what my friend meant, but I also knew that I could be surreptitious in my queries. No one would know what I was looking into. By the time I pulled a copy of Kathleen Norris's *Amazing Grace* off the shelf for my customers, I had almost convinced myself.

THE AFTERNOON BROUGHT in a steady stream of customers and the delight of a visit from Daniel, who had a lull in work for a few minutes and wanted to know if I had time for a walk. Marcus was in for another hour or so, so I let him know I'd be back soon and headed out with Daniel and our two pups.

Walking with two hounds is an exercise in arm strength and patience. I expect some people are able to train their dogs not to tug and pull while they take in the entire planet through their noses, but Daniel and I are not those people. Mayhem required all my body strength to keep her from pulling me off my feet, and Taco, while not as consistently bull-headed as his red-headed counterpart, could follow a scent right into oncoming traffic if Daniel wasn't careful.

The upside of this situation was that a short pass up and back down Main Street meant that the two dogs would be so exhausted when we got back that they'd sleep the rest of the day. The downside was that I would need to see a massage therapist to have the knots in my shoulders worked out. Fortunately, a certain dark-haired mechanic gave a pretty good shoulder rub.

"You heard about Miranda," I said after we'd wrestled the dogs around people and away from discarded trash in silence for a few minutes.

"I did. Saw the sheriff when I dropped off a patrol car after an oil change. That's good news."

"It is." Daniel had come over the night before to sit with Mart and me for a while. He was not happy that we'd gone to her house, of course. But he was even more livid that Rafe would keep tabs on his wife with a doorbell cam.

"I don't wish anyone dead, but that guy, that guy makes me kind of glad he's gone," He had said as he scowled into his hot cocoa.

I couldn't disagree. But I was glad to find out that Miranda hadn't done it. While I knew she would have been justified, maybe even in court, I didn't know if she or those little girls would survive the travails of a court case.

"Now, though, of course, we still have a murderer on our hands. Miranda was the easy suspect given that she stood to inherit her dad's fortune and that she was a long-time domestic violence victim. With her cleared, I'm not sure where to investigate next." As soon as the word *investigate* left my lips, I regretted it.

"Harvey!"

One day I would fully grasp that my friends did not like my new hobby and just not talk about it. But today was not that day.

"Alright, alright, I get it. You and Mart want me to back off."

He put his arm around my waist and pulled me close to him. "We do. Because we care about you. You know that, right?"

"I do." I gave him a little squeeze and started walking again. "I do, but I'm just so fascinated with all these things. Is it okay if we just talk about ideas if I agree not to do anything ridiculous in terms of detective work?"

I could tell that Daniel would rather have dropped the whole idea, but he nodded briskly. "I guess I'd rather be in the loop so I can help if you get into trouble than I would be shut out and have no idea what's happening."

I smiled. "That's my guy." I winked at him and saw him blush. It was the first time I'd use a possessive to describe him. I think he liked it.

"Okay, so who else gains from these two deaths?"

Daniel rolled his eyes but played along. "Do we know that one person killed both of them? I mean what would be the motive? If it was the oil, then wouldn't have someone killed Miranda instead of Rafe?

"You make a good point. Plus, Pickle and Bear were not exactly tight-lipped that they were buying the oil rights, so they would have been the targets, right? I mean if people knew." I gave Mayhem's leash a good tug. "So it's probably not the oil, unless maybe someone thought that they needed to get Rafe out of the way, too. Do you think he would have had access to Miranda's oil fortune?"

Daniel walked in silence for a moment or two. "That's a good question. I think – and you'd know this better than I – that inheritance money isn't split with a spouse. So I don't think Rafe would have had access to the money."

I stopped dead in the middle of the crosswalk. "But does everybody know that? Maybe they thought they had to get Rafe and

Miranda—" I stopped walking. "Oh no, Miranda might still be in danger."

Daniel took my arm and led me out of the street and then waved at the grumpy woman in the red sedan who had been waiting for me to get out of the way. "Could be. But Harvey," he turned and faced me outside of the shop, "that doesn't mean you need to do anything."

"Yes, it does. I need to call Sheriff Mason."

Daniel sighed. "Okay, that you can do. But no snooping."

I gave a weak laugh. "You all must think I'm really nosy."

"We prefer the term *curious*," he said and then gave me a quick kiss on the cheek before we headed back to the shop.

I WAS HALFWAY through dialing when I realized I was doing just what bugged Sheriff Mason so much – assuming he couldn't do his job. If I called him and told him my theory about Miranda still being in danger – a theory he had probably already considered – I'd be insulting him. I definitely didn't want to do that.

Instead, I decided there was no danger in doing a little research myself. I concluded that if I could figure out if Rafe stood to inherit part of the Harris fortune, I'd at least know if someone had motive to kill him specifically. I supposed that other people could be making the same assumption I had – that money in a marriage was always divided equally – but maybe they'd thought to check into that before taking the drastic step of murder.

It was something to look into at least, and I liked having a path to go down, a goal to achieve. It made me feel purposeful.

But my research would have to wait until tomorrow. Marcus's shift was ending, and we had a beautifully full house in the shop. Mart was filling mugs left and right, and almost every reading chair was occupied by a person with a book open. It made my heart feel good.

I wandered the shop and picked up books, putting them on the antique library cart I'd just added to the store's assets. It was made of a beautiful oak that was stained a color somewhere between top soil and sunset. I loved pushing it around the shop to gather the strays from people's shopping endeavors. I thought of all the booksellers and librarians before me who had used the cart. Their fingers had weathered the top a bit, and it felt like I was holding hands with them while I worked. A legacy of books and reading passed down on wheels.

Once I could afford to take the bookshelves to the ceiling and store my overstock there, I planned on installing two or three library ladders in the shop, and then, it would be everything I dreamed. Just a few more big sales, and I'd be there.

I had just finished reshelving and ringing up the day's last customers, when the bell over the door rang. I started to say, "I'm sorry, but we're just closing" when I heard, "Oh, HARVEY!" in the voice of a person I loved dearly.

"Stephen Arritt-Hitchcock?! What are you doing here?"

"Don't forget me, gorgeous," Walter, Stephen's husband said. "Surprise!!"

I couldn't believe it. Stephen and Walter lived in San Francisco, where I had worked with Stephen back in the day. This was no casual drop by on the way home from dinner. They had flown cross-country.

"What are you doing here?" I hugged them both at the same time and took a deep breath. More friends were here, and I was so grateful.

"Mart has been keeping us up on what's happening, and we wanted to be here. This is hard, Harvey."

I wanted to cry, but I needed to keep it together or else I was afraid I would completely fall apart. "Thank you, guys." I gave them another hug. "You're staying with us, right?"

"Well, first, tell me, do you have any bacon?" Walter had a deep love affair with the stuff and ate it almost every morning for breakfast. "You know that the absence of bacon is a deal-breaker." He gave me a grin.

I smirked. "I always keep a pound in the freezer just for you, sir."

"Alright, then, it's settled," Stephen said. "Also, we left our suitcases on your front stoop. The Uber dropped us off there, and then we came right over."

"I see you take nothing for granted." I kissed each of them on the cheek and then finished closing up so we could all go to dinner.

We chose to dine at Chez Cuisine because it was close and, well, open. Most of the restaurants in St. Marin's closed at seven during the week in the off-season because of lack of customers. But Max prided himself on creating as much of a European atmosphere as possible, and apparently, the French ate late. I wouldn't know. I hadn't visited France, and frankly, I wasn't sure Max really knew either. But I was grateful for the chance to drink wine and eat with my friends.

I briefly thought about calling Cate and Lucas, but I decided I'd like a night to just be with three of my oldest friends and even texted Daniel to tell him what was up. He'd totally understood. "Sometimes, you need to reminisce without catching someone up all the time. I'll grab Marcus and order pizza. New *Roadkill* on the DVR."

The man was obsessed with this TV show. In the episode I had watched him, they drove a car across thousands of miles and then put that car's engine into the boat, drove the boat, before putting the engine back in the car and driving home. I had no idea why someone would do such a thing, and when I posited that question to Daniel, he said, "Because they can," which is the reason a lot of us do the things we do, I suppose.

As I entered Chez Cuisine, Max greeted me by, again, taking my hand and kissing it. Then, he looked back at Mart, Stephen, and Walter and said, "Oh, no Daniel. I hope nothing happened." He held onto my hand and moved closer to me. It was creepy.

Mart saved me by looping an arm around my waist and saying, "I'm her date tonight," and then kissing me loudly on the cheek. "Max, we need two bottles of wine, please, one white and one red. You know what I like."

Max blushed, but nodded and headed off.

"He knows what you like?" Walter teased.

Mart smacked him playfully. "What I really meant was, 'Bring me that great bottle of white and that amazing red I just sold you.'"

"Ah, ingesting your own products, I see. That's a testament to how much you believe in what you sell." Stephen pointed to a table in the back, and we slid in. Only one other couple – probably on a first date, if I was reading the body language right – was in the restaurant, so we had our choice of seats.

I nodded and took the seat against the wall. I liked to see what was going on, and for some reason, being tucked in a corner always felt cozy and warm to me.

Max returned with the wine and even went so far as to pour a bit of each for me – why me, I wasn't sure – to sample. I said they were fine. I would have said that for most wine because I didn't really know anything about it, but given that these were from the vineyard where Mart worked, I knew they were good.

Before we even ordered, Max brought out a tray of oysters for the table and an order of the black olive tapenade for me. I loved that stuff and had to restrain myself from eating it right out of the cut-glass bowl with a spoon instead of putting it on the toast bites that Max also brought.

"He's giving us free appetizers?" Mart looked at me.

"Oh, I doubt they're free. But it is odd that he brought them out before we ordered."

"And a little telling that he knew you didn't eat seafood, Harvey." Stephen's voice was full of innuendo.

"What? Wait?! What?! What are you saying? No. No. Nonononono. Don't be ridiculous. It's a small town."

"Uh-huh," Stephen said as he wiggled his eyebrows. "Someone has an admirer." The idea that Max Davies had a thing for me, oh, I didn't like it. Not at all. I mean we got along alright now after our rough start, but he was just kind of smarmy. He always struck me as out to get what was best for him, forget everybody else.

"All I'm saying is that in the ten minutes we've been here, he's kissed your hand, brought you your favorite appetizer, and stared at you nonstop from the door by the kitchen. I think someone has a crush." Walter dropped his voice to a pseudo-whisper. "Want me to go ask him if he likes you?"

I punched my friend in the arm and put my menu in front of my face. "Mart, order for me. You know what I like. I can't look."

"He's coming, Harvey. Put the menu down. You look ridiculous." Mart was teasing, but she also reached over and lowered the menu from my face.

I knew Max had waitstaff – I had just seen a young woman waiting on the other couple – but apparently, we were getting *special* attention. Mart ordered some kind of pork dish, and Stephen and Walter got seafood. But when Max got to me, he said, "I have something just for you, Harvey." He started to turn away but looked back quickly with a smile, "If that's okay."

"Um, sure," I said, and then as soon as he walked away, I whispered, "I'll need frozen pizza when we get home if this goes bad." I shivered. This felt all kinds of icky.

But the food was incredible. Max brought me the most amazing Dijon chicken dish with my favorite mushroom risotto, and I ate every bite. We also finished both bottles of wine and asked for a third to take home. I laughed hard at Walter's jokes and got all the gossip about the fundraising agency where Stephen and I used to work. Aside from Max staying far too close and being much too attentive all evening, it was a beautiful meal.

Stephen and Walter ran interference when it looked like Max was heading our way as we put on our coats to leave. As Mart and I slipped out the door, I heard Stephen say, "So we're thinking of moving to the area. We need to be sure we're here to help with Harvey and Daniel's wedding."

I laughed hard and made a note to thank them, and then as Mart and I sauntered up the block, she got a little sappy from too much stress and too much wine. "So a wedding doesn't sound so bad, huh?"

I really wish a poker face was in my wheelhouse. I looked over at my friend. "It wouldn't be the worst thing."

"What wouldn't?" Stephen said as he and Walter caught up.

"Oh, Harvey was just thinking she'd like you in town to help with the wedding she hopes to have soon."

"Wait!" Walter stopped walking. "Is there talk of a wedding?"

"No. No! And don't you go saying anything to Daniel. We are nowhere near that. I just heard what you said to Max – thank you by the way – and I let myself dream for a minute."

"Well, as I see it, you won't have too long to wait. That guy is totally smitten with you, and in a good way, not in the kind of way that orders for you. Ew," Stephen said with a little shiver.

I smiled at my friend. "Right!?"

"But there was something I wanted to run by you." He slipped his arm through mine. "Walter and I have been talking, and we were wondering, well, if you—"

"Honey, spit it out. Harvey, would it be okay if we also moved to St. Marin's?"

I spun to face the two of them, grabbing Mart close. "Don't tease me, men. Are you serious?"

"As serious as me giving my two weeks' notice yesterday," Stephen said.

"And I sold the business last week," Walter added.

"You quit, you sold. . . . what is happening?" I was bewildered, but in the most delightful way. "You're moving here? You're really moving here?"

"If it's okay with you," Stephen looked a little sheepish.

"Of course it's okay with me. I love it!!" But then I scowled. "But what if I had said no?"

"Then we would have been in trouble," Walter laughed. "We know and love you, though, Harvey, and we knew you'd be in."

"Tomorrow, we start house hunting." Stephen shouted.

"Ooh, I need ALL the pictures." I said as I skipped down the sidewalk backwards.

We stopped into the shop and picked up Mayhem and Taco, who had barely noticed we were gone on their big bed by the register. The dogs were having a sleep over for the first time because I didn't want Daniel to have to come out just to get his pup, and it looked like they had already started without us.

Our little group fell silent as we walked the last few blocks home. As we turned the corner, I said, "So you know there's been a murder?"

Mart sighed. "We almost made it through the night without sleuthing, Harvey." She was teasing, but I could also hear a little edge to her voice. I knew she'd support me in anything I did, but I also knew my endless curiosity was exhausting to her. I had to admit, it was a little exhausting to me, too.

I caught Stephen and Walter up on all the details about Harris' death and then on Rafe's, and I told them about Miranda. They were horrified for her. "Poor woman. Why do abusers do what they do? Is it a cycle of abuse? Passing down of generations? Or something else? Man!"

We walked a bit further. "Tell us how we can help, Harvey. I used my vacation days for the next two weeks, so as of now, we are all yours. I'll have to get a job eventually, but as of tonight, we are officially residents of St. Marin's . . . and your assistant sleuths, if you'll have us."

I grinned. "You mean you're not going back?"

"Well, we'll have to go back in a couple of weeks to pack up, but pretty much, we're here to stay."

"And you'll help me look into Harris's murder?"

Mart groaned. "You two are not helping."

"Sure we are. Call us Harvey's assistant sleuths."

Another groan from Mart . . . and an echo from Taco who was

getting very close to the "carry me" point. We picked up the pace.

We were just turning onto our block when I heard a vehicle start behind us. The street was pretty much empty of cars and people, as usual, so the bright headlights of what must have been a truck shone without obstruction. We kept walking as the truck got closer, but when it didn't pass us, I started to feel the hairs on the back of my neck prickle. Mart grabbed my hand, and I saw Walter drop Stephen's – how awful to worry that your relationship was dangerous.

We started to jog, letting Mayhem and Taco pull us all along. As we sprinted up our driveway, the truck slowed down then stopped before speeding off with a spin of its tires. It was ominous.

I couldn't see the driver or the license plate, but it looked to be an older silver pick-up. Time to call the sheriff. Again.

WE ALL RUSHED INSIDE and locked the door. I dialed the sheriff's office, and the dispatcher said she'd send over a car immediately. "You want me to let the sheriff know, too, Harvey?" she asked.

I paused. I wasn't sure. I knew he'd find out in the morning first thing, and I hated to disturb him this late in his evening. "Nah. The truck is gone, and we're safe. Nothing more he can do before morning anyway."

The officer came by right away and took statements from each of us. Unfortunately, the bright lights of the truck combined with the couple bottles of wine meant none of us could say more than it was a pick-up truck, gray or silver. At least we were consistent in that bit of information.

After the patrol car left with assurances from the office that he'd do a careful scout of the area and then come back through regularly overnight, we settled in with hot cocoa and a fire. Aslan settled her black and white girth on my lap as if she knew I could use the support and found it necessary to show Mayhem the proper way to love a human. The dog would NOT leave my feet and kept licking my hands. Taco had adopted Walter and was draped across his legs in an act of relaxation that was enviable.

"Well, message received, huh?" Mart gave me a pointed look.

"I'd say so, but what message and from whom?" I tried to look innocent, like I wasn't doing the exact opposite of what Mart would like me to do here. I knew she wanted me to drop this, but it felt impossible, especially now.

"Do you guys know that truck?"

I looked at Mart, and she sighed. "No, I don't recognize it. Harvey?"

Sitting back against the cushion and trying not to incur the wrath of the chubby cat, I tried to think about whether I'd seen it before. I felt like I had, but in the dark, I didn't get a good enough look to be sure of that . . . and even if I had, I wasn't recalling why it felt familiar. "Maybe. But I'm not sure."

"The sheriff might know it," Walter said as he dropped another marshmallow in his mug.

"Maybe. But here's my question, why is someone threatening us? I mean the person who had a reason to worry is now dead," I paused as I pictured Rafe's terrifying face in his kitchen, "and I can't think of another person who cared enough about Harris or Rafe to be bothered by my, um, curiosity."

"That's one way to put it," Mart said under her breath and then winked at me.

"I don't know all the details yet," Stephen said, "but there is one person who cared about both of those men, right?"

Mart and I locked eyes. "Miranda."

The air in the room got heavy. None of us, not even Stephen and Walter who only heard her story, wanted that idea to be true, but it sounded, again, like the most likely suspect was Miranda.

"But wait a minute," Mart stood up. "Surely Miranda doesn't drive an old pick-up, right? We saw her SUV in her garage, remember?"

I sat forward. "True. But she could have hired someone."

Mart looked out of the top of her eyes at me. "What reason would Miranda have to send someone to intimidate—Oh, right." She sat back down.

"Right, if she thinks we're getting close . . . I can't imagine it, especially after what she's been through. It seems like she's barely getting through the day – at least I know that's how I would be." I sat back and rubbed my hands over my face. "But I can't say we rule her out, I guess."

Walter sat forward. "I don't like the idea either, Harvey, but how else would anyone know you were there yesterday? I mean, why would anyone else have any reason to feel threatened by your, er, inquiries?"

Walter had a point, but I had hit the wall. I couldn't think about it anymore. I needed to get some sleep and let my subconscious mind do the work while my conscious one dreamed of gorgeous libraries lined with jewel-toned books and not a body in sight.

THE NEXT MORNING, I was awake before anyone else, well, except for Taco, who seemed to think that six a.m. was a reasonable time to scratch on my door and ask for both a bathroom break and a snack. I was one of those people who could not get back to sleep if awakened any time after five a.m., so I put on my fluffy Doctor Who robe, let Taco into the fenced backyard, and made my way to the coffeepot. I was always grateful that either Mart or I premade the coffee before we went to bed every night, but this morning I was especially grateful. I had slept hard, but not well. I kept dreaming of pick-up trucks slamming into my store. It was not a restful night.

Taco knocked at the French doors, and I let him in and fed him and Mayhem, who had peeled herself off the dog bed by the fireplace to eat before immediately returning to her warm spot. Aslan, apparently sensing that the dogs were going back to bed, joined me in the kitchen, and I gave her a little treat of the horrible-smelling cat food that I kept for special occasions like the administration of medicine. But she'd slept curled against the back of my knees all night and was what grounded me each time I woke. I owed her.

The menagerie fed, I took myself to my favorite reading chair – a wing-backed antique covered in a paisley upholstery woven from the most brilliant reds, purples, greens, and blues. In some homes, it would look outright garish, but here, it was lovely against all our wood tones and book spines.

I wrapped up in the crazy quilt Mart had made for me three years ago in her quilting phase – we were in the time of the wood-carving now – and picked up my latest read, *Out of the Silent Planet* by C.S. Lewis. It was the first book in his space trilogy, and I was loving it. I'd read the third one, *That Hideous Strength*, for a class back in college, but this was my first time to try the whole trilogy, and I was not disappointed.

As I read about Ransom's escape from his captors and pondered the idea that to save some you might have to sacrifice one, I felt it, that tiny sense that my brain was onto something but wasn't quite ready to let me in on the secret yet. I kept reading, confident my mind would clue me in when necessary.

By the time the rest of the humans in the house started to rouse about eight, I was more relaxed than I'd been when I woke. Reading always did that for me – took me out of my own head and gave me a space to float apart.

When I heard showers start up, I got out the griddle, opened the bacon that I'd thawed overnight, and started to cook. As Mart, Stephen, and Walter each made their way to the kitchen, I served them bacon, eggs, and coffee, made to order for each of my dearest friends.

The silence around the kitchen island made me smile, and I pattered off in my slippers to get my own shower. By the time I'd tamed my wild hair and gotten back to the kitchen, it was spotless, and I knew I'd gotten the best end of that deal. I hated trying to clean all the dots of bacon grease that mysteriously appeared whenever I cooked that deliciousness.

Mart headed out to the winery with a promise to be back in time for dinner at Cate and Lucas's house, and I walked into town with Stephen, Walter, Taco, and Mayhem, where the two men would meet up with their real estate agent and the two dogs and I would head into the bookstore. I kind of wished the pooches could run the shop today, and I'd curl up in one of the armchairs and play their role. But alas, the no-opposable-thumbs situation made that untenable.

I had just gotten the shop ready – cash to the register, door unlocked, open sign on – when Sheriff Mason came in, and he didn't look happy. Specifically, he didn't look happy with me.

Trying to lighten the mood, I said, "That looks like the face of a man who needs a cup of coffee."

He grunted. Literally grunted. This was not going well.

"Well, I need coffee. Do you mind?"

A brisk nod was my only permission, so I scooted over to the café and poured a big mug of Rocky's dark roast while giving her the universal of shrug of "I have no idea."

Back at the counter, the sheriff looked a little less peeved, and I took a deep breath and a long sip before I said, "So the truck?"

Apparently, I broke the seal on his frustration because he let it all out. "Harvey Beckett, I have told you time and time again that your snooping would bring trouble. You KNOW it brings trouble, and yet over and over, you put your nose where it can get chopped off."

"I know. I'm sorry. I was just trying to make things easier for you—"

"Oh, that's rich. You think it's *easier* for me if I'm having to chase down trucks that threaten to run people down. That makes my job easier? More work makes my job easier?" His voice was getting louder and louder.

I stood up a little straighter and took another sip. I didn't want to cry, and I didn't want to shout back, especially since a couple of customers had just come in. Coffee seemed the best option.

"You're right," I said. "I'm sorry."

He stared at me, "And . . ."

"And nothing. I screwed up."

He kept staring.

"Really. I'm done. No more sleuthing. I quit."

"Okay, then." He put his hands behind his neck and leaned back. "Now, tell me about this truck."

I repeated all we knew – silver, older model, not exactly pristine.

"But no one saw the license plate or the driver?"

"No. None of us did. We'd had a couple of bottles of wine, and he'd been following us so our eyes were a little wonky from his lights."

He was writing all this down in his notebook, and so I had a minute to think. I figured since I really was serious about not sleuthing anymore, I probably needed to just tell him that we had thought maybe Miranda could still be guilty.

"Sheriff, after the truck incident last night, the four of us were talking – you know, just trying to calm down and figure out what had just happened. I guess maybe it's natural to just want to figure out who scared you so badly and why . . ." I paused to get my breath.

"And you came back to Miranda, thought I might have missed something."

I winced. I hadn't thought of it like that. "It just seemed like she had the most reason, and since Mart and I screwed up so bad with her the other day . . ."

He sighed. "The thought had occurred to me, too. But I have no evidence, and to be honest, it just seems unlikely to me." He looked me in the eye. "I think you know what I mean."

"I do. Something just feels like she's not to blame for this."

He slid his notebook into his shirt pocket. "I agree. But I have to follow the evidence. I will keep you posted, Harvey, as a courtesy. But you have to stay out of things okay? Really?"

"Really. I hear you, Tucker. And I really am sorry."

He squeezed my forearm. "I hear we're going to have new residents of St. Marin's."

I grinned. "I may never get used to how quickly word travels in this town."

He laughed. "I hear that. Well, tell Stephen and Walter welcome for me."

As he walked out the door, I turned to see who had come in while we were talking and found Pickle and Bear glowering at me from the poetry section. This didn't look good.

8

I took a deep breath in preparation for what was going to be, apparently, my second difficult conversation during my first cup of coffee. "Gentlemen, what can I do you for?"

Bear growled. Literally growled, and I took a step back. Then he cracked up laughing.

"Nothing, Harvey," Pickle said. "We heard about what happened last night and just wanted to stop by and show our support."

"After breakfast, of course. You do know that the gas station just north of town has the best bacon, egg, and cheese biscuits on the Eastern Shore, don't you?" Bear patted his stomach.

I laughed. "I was not aware of that, but I do hear the one south of town has the best fried chicken in the State."

Pickle cackled. "Darn tootin'. We do love our gas station food." He straightened his tie. "Seriously, though, Harvey, that's serious business, that truck and all. You don't live alone do you?"

Bear nudged him. "Not if Daniel has anything to say about it."

I blushed. "Actually, I don't live alone. My roommate is named Martha; we call her Mart. She works here sometimes when she's not over at the winery."

"Oh, yes, pretty thing, long dark hair?"

That pretty much described Mart perfectly. "That's her. She's my roommate. And right now, my friends—" I cleared my throat. These two guys seemed great, but sometimes *great* disappeared when the word *gay* entered the conversation, "are staying with us while they house hunt, too."

"Right. I'd forgotten about Stephen and Walter. Nice men. Their real estate agent contacted me just to give me a heads up that I'd probably need to make time for a closing soon," Pickle said.

"Oh good." I nodded, and from the gentle gleam in Pickle's eye, I could tell he knew I meant more than, *Oh good, you're handling the closing.*

"Always great to have good folks moving into town," Bear followed up as he tugged on his suspenders. "Anyway, Harvey, we just wanted you to know we've got you. Call us if you need anything." Each of them handed me a business card. "Our cell numbers are on the back. Day or night."

I took the cards and slid them into the back pocket of my jeans. "Thank you, gentlemen. That means the world to me."

I gave them each a little pat on the shoulder as they walked past me to the front door.

I barely had time to get the rest of my first cup of coffee in before Woody walked in. "You okay, Harvey?"

"I am, Woody. Thank you. How did *you* hear?"

He looked up at the ceiling for a minute. "I think it was at breakfast. Homer mentioned it."

"Let me guess. At the gas station north of town?"

"Best biscuits on the Eastern Shore."

"So I've heard." I waved him along as I headed back to the café with my mug. "I guess it's pretty much common knowledge now, huh?"

"Yep, but that's probably a good thing. People will keep an eye out for you."

I laughed. "Pickle and Bear were just in to say that very thing. Can I ask you a question, though, Woody?" I knew I was treading a thin line here what with my word to the sheriff and all, but I couldn't stop myself.

"Do you know who drives an older silver pick-up? I don't know anything about cars, but maybe something from the '70s?"

Woody poured enough sugar into his coffee to make the spoon stand up and then said, "Nope, I don't. That the truck that came after you?"

"Yeah. Guess that detail hadn't made it out yet? Maybe keep it to yourself then? I don't want to get in the way of the sheriff's investigation."

"You got it, girl." He lifted his to-go cup in my direction. "Thanks for the coffee."

"Any time. You know it's always on the house here, Woody, as thanks for all the fixtures." Woody had made our sign, benches for the front of the shop, and now he was working on window boxes to go on the mural I was having painted on the side of the building next to the garden center. It would look like windows into the store, and I thought adding actual window boxes would be a funky, fun bit.

"Much appreciated, Harvey. Have a good one." He saluted me with his coffee cup and went out the door.

For a moment, as I watched Woody walk up the road, I thought about what it would have been like to have a dad like him, a man who built you a playhouse as big as his workshop when you were a little girl. A man who flew cross-country for Thanksgiving only to build you bookshelves when he arrived. A man who wanted to build his daughter a sign for her dream business. But I didn't have that father, and so I figured I better just be grateful I had Woody as a bonus.

I fluttered my lips with a long breath and turned back to the shop. We weren't having a major event in the store this weekend, but still, we were always busier on Saturday and Sunday, and what with the summer tourist season just starting to get into gear, I wanted to be sure everything was in tip-top shape.

I spent the morning restocking our shelves with the shipment of our primary stock that had arrived the evening before. I faced out some books that I loved and some Marcus did, too, and I texted Mart, Josie, and Daniel for their new "staff" picks. Marcus came in at eleven and put up his own titles – *To Kill A Mockingbird* and *In Cold Blood*, a genius combination that was sure to be a conversation starter when people learned that Lee and Capote were lifelong friends. My choices were *Hiawatha and the Peacemaker* by Robbie Robertson, a gorgeous picture book, and *City of Ghosts* by V.E. Schwab, a really fun and just-a-touch-scary YA book.

By the time I got everyone's selections and finished the display, we had a beautiful array of titles that ranged from psychology to art to the newest fiction. I loved it, and I thought our customers would, too. In fact, as soon as I walked away, someone came to browse and ended up buying one of Lucas's titles, *Stamped from the Beginning*.

This job never got old. I loved seeing people find books they found fascinating, and I loved watching books go out the door. I also loved watching books come in the door. Also buying books.

I clearly had a hard-core case of bibliophilia, and I was fine with that.

At noon, I waved to Marcus as Taco, Mayhem, and I headed to Daniel's garage. We'd texted a bit since Stephen and Walter had come to town, but I really wanted to catch him up on everything, especially the incident with the pick-up truck. But when I arrived, he had a customer in his office, so I gave him a wave and then tried to lift Taco so he could wave, too. This proved to be impossible given the Basset's girth, so I dipped his paw in a tiny spot of oil and left a signed note from the pup to his owner saying we'd see him at closing for dinner.

Then, with time to kill and a hankering for some street food, the pups and I went in search of Lu and her amazing taco truck. A search in St. Marin's is not hard, and I found her just up the block, parked beside Elle's farm stand, and by some miracle, she didn't have a line. I tied the dogs to the light post and dragged over the water bowl that Lu always left out for canine passersby and went to get my carnitas fix.

Lu, short for Luisa, was Sheriff Mason's wife, and she made the most amazing tacos I'd ever tasted. Full of flavor, not a bit dry, and delightfully messy. When I reached the window, she exclaimed, "Harvey!" and then leaned down through the tiny window to give me a hug with her wrists. "One, no, two carnitas coming up."

"How did you know I wanted two today, Lu?"

She smiled and said, "Anyone who stares down a truck in the middle of the night deserves two tacos!" As she turned to the griddle, she said, "You're okay, right?" Her voice was more serious now. "Tucker told me what happened."

I sighed. "I am okay. Still a bit shaken, but okay. Thanks for asking."

"I know Tucker is worried about you." She gave me a conspiratorial grin. "And I know you are curious, no?"

I laughed. "I was warned about my curiosity by your husband just this morning." I looked around as if making sure he wasn't nearby. "But, yes. Yes, I am very curious. I just can't stop thinking about who would have killed Huckabee and Rafe. The motive just doesn't make sense."

Lu handed me my tacos with a snicker. "You sound just like my husband. Motive – people kill people all the time for lots of reasons. I know that Tucker is trying to investigate the money, but maybe it wasn't about the money."

"Hmm. I'll have to give that some thought . . . but just thought, mind you. I promised the sheriff no more sleuthing for me."

"I'll believe it when I see it," Lu said. "Thanks for coming, Harvey. On the house. I need you to order some more books for me. I'll come by later in the week."

Lu regularly ordered the latest cookbooks as well as a fair selection of steamy romances, and I was always happy to accommodate her, especially since I loved learning about books I didn't know much about.

I lifted my plate in salute. "Thanks, Lu."

As I spun around to find a quiet corner where I could gobble down this goodness, I went face-first into a chest. I took a step back and looked up into the beard of Homer Sloan. "Oh, hi," I said with a flush. "Sorry, I didn't see you there."

He stepped back and said, "Hi, Harvey. Good to see you." He looked tired, very tired. The bags under his eyes were carrying luggage.

"You okay?" I asked as I balanced my plate of tacos and took a look to be sure the dogs were still good. Apparently, they were fine – sound asleep back to back on the sidewalk in a sunbeam.

"Sure, why?" His voice had that false cheer of fatigue and effort. "I'll take what she has, Lu," he said to the window.

I was a bit puzzled by what felt like a little defensiveness in his tone, but I shrugged it off in the hopes of getting to my tacos while they were still piping hot. "Just making small talk. I imagine you've got a lot more work over at the ranch now." I paused and tilted my head. "Although maybe Huckabee wasn't much of a hands-on manager, and you're still doing the same old same old."

He smiled slightly. "More or less. But now I'm managing the business side of things, too, until Miranda gets her feet under her and can take over."

"Oh, right. Miranda will take over. I hadn't thought about that." I silently wondered what she would need to be ready. A lot of support that's for sure. "Well, I'm glad she has you to help her keep things going and then guide her when she steps in. I expect you've helped her broker that deal with Pickle and Bear."

Now I was sure that Homer was more than just tired. He looked downright angry. "Nope, I can't say as I did." His words were clipped and sharp. "She made that decision all on her own."

"Oh, I see. Well, it sounds like it might be a good idea, keep her steady while she gets a fresh start. I know she's glad to have you." I didn't know exactly what was going on with Homer today, but flattery almost never failed.

"Here you go, Homer," Lu said.

As he turned to take his tacos, I saw a little blush go up his cheeks. Flattery worked every time. "Anyway, I'm off to devour these goodies. Good to see you, Homer." I waved a foil-wrapped delight in his general direction and received a similar salute in return.

I decided to head back to the shop and hide in the backroom with my lunch and a large supply of napkins . . . that is if I could keep the hounds from grabbing the tacos right out of my hands before we got there.

BY LATE AFTERNOON, I could feel the effects of all the week's excitement catching up with me, and I needed caffeine. Once again, I was glad Marcus was on hand. I was dragging, but he had some real Air Jordan-powered pep in his step today. I wanted to ask him if he'd gotten some good news or something, but I was just too tired.

Still, his presence in the store had definitely been good in a number of ways. I was especially delighted to see more young people – that's how I thought of them, even though that kind of thinking made me feel ancient – coming in. The number of teenagers and college students spending time in the shop was definitely increasing, and, just now, Marcus was showing a slightly squealy group of teenage girls our YA section and talking about how much he loved *Trail of Lightning* by Rebecca Roanhorse. I had no doubt I'd need to restock that title if the girls' swoony eyes and small touches on Marcus's arm were any indication of potential purchases.

I gave him a little wave and a wink as I entered the café and took a seat near the counter so Rocky and I could chat while I caffeinated.

"You okay, Harvey? You look – sorry – like you've been drained of blood by a vampire."

I chuckled. "I bet I do. That might have been easier than my week actually, especially if the vampire was sparkly."

She laughed, but then leaned onto the counter to look me in the eye. "Really, though, Harvey. Are you okay? This week has been, well, a lot."

I sank back against the wall next to me and sighed. "I am. I mean, I think I am. I'm better than I was on Tuesday after visiting Miranda. That was so hard – so sad and so scary. But now, now, I'm just run-down. It's nice to have a pretty normal day today."

Rocky smiled. "Agreed. No one over here has asked for me to toast their cookie or anything."

"Seriously?"

"Yep, this one guy. Every time."

I rolled my eyes. "People." I took a long swig of my coffee and let my shoulders drop a bit.

"How about you? Your week started kind of rough with your car and all. Is it getting better? How's the final exam prep going?"

Rocky's face flushed a little. "Daniel told you what happened, didn't he?" When I nodded, she continued quietly, "I was so embarrassed, but he was so nice, Harvey. Didn't even tease me."

I smiled. "I think he's actually one of those nice guys."

"You think?"

"Okay, well, I know." I lowered my voice a little. "I don't mean to pry, but if you need cash or something . . ." I let my sentence trail off.

Rocky swallowed hard. "Harvey, that is so sweet. No, I'm fine. Actually better than I have been for a while because of this café. Sales have been good, and the profit-sharing is working well. Thanks for that." She looked out the window over my left shoulder. "No, Monday wasn't about money. I was, um, distracted."

My first thought was that she had been thinking about school, but something about the tentativeness in her voice told me something more was going on. "Oooh. Do you want to talk about this distraction?"

Her eyes darted over to the register where a certain young man was selling all our copies of Roanhorse's fantasy novel.

"OH," I said. "Really?"

She shrugged and smiled. "I think so. I mean, we've been out a couple of times."

I didn't know why I hadn't seen it before – all the trips Marcus took to the café only to return without a coffee mug. I never came back from the café without coffee. I was delighted though. I liked when good people found other good people. "I love this, Rocky. That's awesome."

"We're keeping it pretty quiet. Don't want pressure and stuff."

"Got it. I won't stay a word to him . . . or to you, if you'd like, unless you bring it up. No pressure from me." I smiled at her. "But it does look like you're happy, and that makes me happy."

She blushed again, and I gave her hand a pat as I headed back to work.

DINNER THAT NIGHT was the perfect combination of frivolity and companionship that I needed. We all gathered at Cate and Lucas's place after the shop closed – me, Daniel, Mart, Marcus, Rocky, Stephen, and Walter – for a crab boil. Okay, for me it was one of Lucas's amazing hamburgers, but for everyone else, it was a massive pile of crabs, potatoes, and corn on the cob poured onto brown paper that was spread end-to-end on their dining room table.

Basically, the idea was that everyone sat around the table and cracked open crab shells with their bare hands and a communal claw cracker. Cate was wise and had put a small trashcan next to each seat, and so instead of the massive pile of crab shells and spent corn cobs that I'd seen at other boils, the table got more and more clear as my friends ate. And ate. And ate. It was impressive, really.

Stephen and Walter, crab boil novices, were especially fun to watch since they went all in with total gusto even though they had no idea what they were doing. By the time they came up for air, they were covered in little bits of crab meat and Old Bay and looked blissful, if slightly uncomfortable from overeating.

I, however, had not overeaten, and so when Lucas brought out his famous cupcakes, I did not have to wait until dinner settled, especially since I'd finished dinner thirty minutes earlier than everyone else. Instead, I got my pick – the lemon meringue cupcake – and even had time to get my second choice – carrot with cream cheese frosting – before anyone else was ready for firsts. There were advantages to not eating seafood in a water-side town.

After everyone finished, we all waddled into the living room and sat on their giant sectional to watch *Ferris Bueller's Day Off*. For most of us, it was an act of nostalgia. For Rocky and Marcus it was, apparently, an act of horror. "Look at how awful the stunts look." "Those jeans are terrible." "Did people really talk like that?"

At first, those of us for whom Matthew Broderick's performance was epic and part and parcel with our childhood were – okay, I – it was only me – was put off by the snide comments coming from the younger corner of the sofa, but by the end of the movie, we were all laughing at the ridiculousness which we had all known was there even back in the day. Sometimes, it's best to let a hero topple.

After the movie, we helped clean up the last of our mess, making sure that Mayhem, Taco, and Cate and Lucas's miniature Schnauzer, Sasquatch, got a few bits of crab as a treat. We hadn't talked about anything serious, and we'd all carefully avoided talking about the murders. I thought I might have been frustrated by the distraction – I like things resolved and as quickly as possible – but in fact, I felt more relaxed than I had in days.

Marcus had offered to escort Rocky to her car, and when Daniel had almost offered to walk with them, I'd given him a kick under the table. He shot me a look, but kept his mouth shut. The stroll back through town was quiet, and I enjoyed looking at the tulips under the moonlight as I walked with the people I loved most in the world through the town we'd now all be calling home. I was looking forward to lots of years with these people, but I was also excited to get a good night's sleep for the first time in a few days.

Then, we saw my parents' car in our driveway, and all the tension came flooding back.

I had forgotten I'd given them a key a few days earlier just in case they needed to get into the house. Apparently, they had "needed" to get in because when we got inside, they were both asleep on the couch, presumably because they had seen Stephen and Walter's belongings in our only guest room.

Mom's lower legs dangled over the edge of the loveseat, and Dad was stretched out with his face to the back of the sofa. But while Dad had won the space lottery, Mom had taken the prize for blankets. Dad was under a single sheet – I would not tell them that was Aslan's sheet, the one she used to make a bed wherever in the house she so desired. Dad would be covered in black and white fur when he woke up. Mom, however, was under the quilt from my reading chair and an afghan she'd pilfered from the foot of my bed. For a minute, I wondered why they hadn't lit the fire since it was a chilly night, but the box of matches next to the auto-lighting gas fireplace gave me my answer.

In that moment, I felt pretty tender to them, there on our sofas, sleeping. I decided to hold on to that feeling until morning and gave Daniel a gentle kiss before watching him and Taco go up the drive toward home and turning to see my dear friends quietly retiring to their own rooms. I felt at peace for the first time in a long time.

9

*T*he next morning, I woke from a beautifully good sleep and managed to stay peaceful even when I heard my mother's voice in the kitchen. "I cannot make this coffee. It comes pre-ground in a huge bag. Who buys coffee like this?"

"Apparently, our daughter buys coffee like this, honey." I could almost see him smoothing a hair back from her face. "I'll buy you real coffee in town. For now, let's just do this thing and make the kids breakfast."

"The kids." I sighed. That was how they saw me, wasn't it? Still their kid. There was that tender feeling again. I couldn't decide if I liked it or not.

I took a quick look at myself in the mirror and despaired. This hair was going to garner some commentary, but I just couldn't care this morning. Honestly, I simply wanted to be with mom and dad. So I took a deep breath, pulled the tie on my Doctor Who robe tight, and went in.

To my mom's credit, she did not say anything about my hair – she gave it a long, withering look, but she did not speak. Instead, she held her arms wide open and pulled me into a hug. Then, I went to Dad and hugged him, too. Classic Beckett behavior here – pretend like everything is alright, even when it's not. Still, I was not yet ready to talk about our falling out from earlier in the week.

"Did I hear something about breakfast?" I asked with what I hoped sounded like child-like enthusiasm.

"You did, kiddo. Pancakes with blueberries *and* chocolate chips sound good?" Dad was already at the griddle with spatula in hand.

That had been my favorite breakfast as a child. Okay, my *favorite* favorite was minus the blueberries, but this was the compromise my family came to – chocolate and fresh fruit. "Yes, sir. I'd love that. Can we make enough for six? Mart is home, and Stephen and Walter are staying with us for a few days while they house hunt."

Mom smacked her hand on the counter. "Well, I love that. They're moving to town. How wonderful." She smiled. "And I know you'll love having them here, won't you? Especially with all this—"

"Sharon, maybe we can save the hard stuff for after pancakes?" Dad's voice had just the touch of a whine to it.

"No, it's okay, Dad." I climbed up onto a barstool. "I really am glad they're moving here, especially with all the goings on lately. I guess it must had made the Baltimore papers."

Mom sat down next to me and let Dad take over the pancake mix she'd been making from memory. "It did. Did you know that Lewis fellow?"

"I met him once." I shuddered. "He was pretty awful."

"So we gathered," Dad said as he cracked an egg. "I guess he was a wife beat—Sorry, an abuser is the more appropriate term, I think."

"He was. We saw his handiwork, Mart and I."

"Oh honey." Mom put her hand on mine. "So you know his wife?"

"Only a little. But she and her daughters have been in the shop. They're wonderful girls."

Mart came out of the back and stretched. She, unlike me, looked like she'd just stepped out of a mattress advertisement. Her hair was perfect, and she didn't have even a single sleep wrinkle. Sigh. "Did I hear something about pancakes?"

"How many do you want, girl?" Dad said. "One? Two?"

"Are you kidding me?" She looked at me. "Is he kidding? Clearly, Mr. Beckett, you have not seen me eat pancakes. Make mine a six-pack please. Heavy on the chocolate," she said as she scooped a few chips from the bag on the counter.

"She looks like a model, but she eats like a lumberjack. My kind of woman," Dad said as he winked at Mom.

I laughed. This felt good. Really good. But still, I braced myself for this sweet familial moment to dissolve at any moment. I hated that I wasn't able to just enjoy this time, but past experience with my parents made me leery.

A few minutes later, Stephen and Walter came in, freshly showered and shaved, and they did exactly what my dad expected them to do, go to him for a firm handshake. They followed that up with a strong but short hug for mom. I wondered if there was some school that taught people how to be good children. If so, I probably needed to go.

But despite my slight wariness, breakfast was delightful. We ate gathered around the island and used far too much syrup for our pancakes. The conversation was light and centered on what the Arritt-Hitchcocks were looking for in their new home – water view, lots of light, a home office. When all of the pancakes were devoured – Mart conquered her small monument to carbs without a problem – we worked together to clean up. Then, Mom and Dad used my bathroom and bedroom to get ready for the day, and I tucked my clothes under my arm like I was in college again and trotted over to Mart's space to do the same.

By nine fifteen, we were all loaded up in Mart's car and Mom and Dad's car to caravan to the shop. We'd all decided we wanted to visit this house that Stephen and Walter had seen the day before and really loved. I just needed to stop by work to be sure everything was set, and then we'd be off for a rendezvous with their real estate agent.

Of course, Marcus and Rocky had the shop well in hand, and from the quiet smiles they were giving each other across the shop, it looked like they were relishing the chance to run the store alone. I, for one, was relishing the gift of letting them, and climbed back into Mart's car with a flourish.

"Feels good to have help, doesn't it?" Mart said as she pulled away from the curb to follow Walter, who Dad had trusted to drive his brand new Tesla.

I smiled. "Always. I just wish I was better at accepting it."

She didn't look over at me, but I saw a small smile grace her lips.

I squeezed her arm and said, "You have time for this? I know Saturdays are busy at the winery."

"They are, but we discourage drinking before noon by not open-ing. I'll be there late tonight to prep for a wedding tomorrow on-site, so it's fine if I get in a little later. I'm dying to see this house."

Mart and I had hoped to find a little place on the water when we'd moved the fall before, but our budget and my desire to be within walking distance of work didn't make that feasible. The places we could afford on the water in town came with room-mates of the rodent and reptile variety. No thank you.

But having Stephen and Walter get a place on the water, that was basically the next best thing. As we drove out of town, I slipped into visions of having evenings on their pier with a Mai Tai in my hand. Never mind that I had never had a Mai Tai and had no idea what was in one, but it felt luxurious. Especially if it had an umbrella.

I was so deep in my reverie that I almost missed it when we passed the gates to the Harris ranch. I lurched forward, scaring Mart, as I tried to get a better look inside. "Gracious, Harvey. What's going on?" she asked.

I sat back. "That was the Harris place. I was just trying to get a peek."

She snuck a look at me out of the corner of her eye, but then turned on her signal and followed Walter into the next driveway down 33. The house Walter and Stephen liked was next door to the Harris' place. Excitement and foreboding settled on me, even though next door out here meant that there was almost a mile between driveways.

I quickly decided not to say anything further – I didn't want anyone distracted by the loose, geographical connection to the murders, and I didn't want to distract myself by pondering what this might mean for more sleuthing.

Fortunately, the house was so gorgeous I didn't have to worry. It was a brand-new build with dusky blue siding with white trim and a small set of stairs leading to a front porch that was perfect for a potted plant and a shoe rack to keep people from tracking sand into the house – Stephen and Walter had been influenced by the Chinese culture of San Francisco and preferred everyone remove their shoes when coming in, even when sand wasn't involved. They had a beautiful array of slippers for guests, and frequent visitors got their own pair. Mine were leopard print with hot-pink fuzz because my friends thought they were hilarious. Hot pink is *not* my preference in anything but icing.

We took a walk around the outside of the house while we waited for the real estate agent to arrive, and I stopped short on the water side of the building. It was almost all windows in a not-quite symmetrical layout that somehow gave the house a feeling of balance against the gentle curve of the shoreline below. The house was relatively private, with tall trees on each side to create a screen from the neighbors.

But the water, the water was the real showstopper. The brackish waters were deep aqua, and the pier was wide, perfect for fishing and sitting. With a Mai Tai of course.

I could barely wait to get inside, and when the agent came and unlocked the house, I was not disappointed. The front door opened into a small foyer and then beyond was a huge room with a fireplace centered on that wall of windows looking over the water. The view was so spectacular that it took me a while to look around the rest of the space.

But when I did, I knew this was the future home of Stephen and Walter Arritt-Hitchcock. From the chef's kitchen to the charming guest bedrooms and bathroom just off the living space to the master suite upstairs that was a loft but with a beautiful, sliding wall of frosted glass for more privacy, it was gorgeous. Just enough space for them to enjoy, but not so much that they'd be overwhelmed by their own desire to keep their residence pristine.

I knew the house had to cost far more than I could afford – I had avoided the real estate apps out of respect for my friends' privacy – but they were selling their house in The Haight in San

Francisco. Let's just say they probably could have bought two of these houses for what they'd get for that one property on the West Coast.

We all wandered the house for a while, opening cabinet doors and closets, snooping with abandon since it was new construction and we weren't violating anyone's privacy (although let's be honest, I might have opened everything anyway.) The agent was remarkably gracious, especially since we had crashed her showing and were not shy with our questions about everything from HOAs to noise ordinances. (Mayhem was not always good at using her inside voice, and I knew she'd be visiting a lot, especially after I convinced Stephen and Walter to get a miniature Pomeranian named Lola – a pet I desperately wanted someone else to own.)

By the time we went back outside, I was convinced they should buy, and from the way my two friends were talking quietly throughout the house, it seemed they were, too. I distinctly heard a "our sectional will fit perfectly here" comment from Walter.

Back in the driveway, Mart took off for work, and Mom, Dad, and I told Stephen and Walter we were going to take a stroll up the road so that they could have some time with their agent. I was actually glad to have a moment to talk to my parents alone. I had avoided the hard conversation long enough. I needed to apologize.

We hung a right onto 33 and kept to the shoulder to give the traffic plenty of space to go around us. "That house is gorgeous, isn't it?" I asked, warming up to the harder topic.

"Amazing," Mom said. "Those windows."

I nodded. "I can't wait to sit in there and watch thunderstorms."

"I was thinking the same thing," Mom said. "The lightning on the water." We had watched a lot of storms from our Baltimore front porch when I was a kid. It was one of the few times we were peacefully together.

The silence started to feel heavy as we walked, and I started to say, "Mom, I'm sorry—" at the exact same moment, she said, "I'm sorry, Harvey."

We looked at each other and each chuckled nervously. "I am sorry, Mom. You were right. I lied, and that wasn't a kind thing to do."

"And I'm sorry for not being more thoughtful about your time. We should have let you know we were coming and worked with your schedule." She looked down at her hands and then over at me. "We did it again this time, but I just couldn't handle the way we'd left things."

Mom reached over and took my hand, and I felt the tears pool in my eyes. She had not held my hand in a very long time. I gave her fingers a squeeze.

"I haven't been," she looked over at Dad, "we haven't always been very good at understanding what you do and why you do it. You're very different than I am. I know you know that. You just don't want the same things I want, the things I wanted for you. It's taken me a long time to realize that. I'm sorry."

I was crying for real now. "I'm sorry, too, Mom. I tried for a long time to be the person you wanted me to be, and I was wrong to do that, but not because what you want is bad. It's not. It's just not me. Maybe if I'd been honest more often, it wouldn't have taken us this long to understand each other."

My dad scooted closer and put his arm around my shoulder. "I'm sorry, too," he whispered. My dad wasn't a man who used words frivolously, so his apology, as brief as it was, made me cry even harder.

Eventually, though, my tears stopped, and I enjoyed the stroll. It was only when I started looking around that I realized we'd wandered to Huckabee Harris's place. I knew Daniel would probably note that my subconscious was sleuthing, but I really hadn't made a conscious choice at all. We'd just ended up here, by the gate, the gate that only blocked cars but not people on foot because, really, who walks all the way out here.

I shot Stephen a text to see how they were doing.

"Writing up an offer. You okay?" he replied.

"Just fine. Enjoying our walk. Take your time."

I looked at my mom and dad who were admiring the very impressive, very sturdy, very tall gate in front of us and asked, "Who's up for a little sleuthing?"

Mom and Dad looked at each other and grinned. "We do have this in common."

"What, nosiness?"

"I like to call it *curiosity*," Mom said, and I laughed. We had that in common, too, I guess.

For a minute, it felt like we were in one of those films where a group of heroes walks forward slowly while a wind blows our hair. The breeze off the water wasn't quite as dramatic, but as we all moved toward the gate, I imagined us snapping gloves into place and brandishing our weapons.

My fantasy dissolved a bit when I tripped over the scrub brush around the gate, but still, within seconds, we walked onto Harris's driveway. I didn't think anyone would even notice us, but if they did, the "they" was probably going to be Homer, and I could just tell him the truth – that we'd been visiting the house next door with friends and thought we'd stop over.

As we walked, I caught Mom and Dad up on what had

happened since they were here last. Dad was very unhappy that Mart and I had gone over to see Miranda, but Mom came to my defense. "Burt, what was she supposed to do? She couldn't let that poor woman suffer if there was any way she could help." I gaped at my mother for a few seconds, pleasantly surprised at her compassion, but made sure to study my face back to serious before she caught me. No need to destroy our shaky peace and tenderness.

Rafe's death puzzled them, though. "But neither you nor the sheriff thinks Miranda killed him?" Dad said.

"No. I know she seems the most likely suspect – and I wouldn't blame her at all if she'd done it – but no one thinks she did. But then, that leaves us without a real suspect."

"Right." Mom was pensive. "But isn't she the one that falsely accused that young man Marcus of killing her father?"

I had totally forgotten about the way she'd attacked Marcus because I was focusing on her suffering at the attacks of her husband. Ugh. I had to apologize to Marcus for that when I got back. "Yes, that's right. That was her." Now I had another curveball to figure out. "Why would she do that?"

"The obvious reason is that she committed the murder and was looking to draw attention away from herself," Dad said. He was clearly not as quick to accept Miranda's innocence, and while I didn't like it, I wondered if his willingness to believe her a killer might not be a good thing. It might just push us to study the angles a bit more.

"That's true," Mom's voice was thoughtful. "Or maybe she was trying to draw attention away from someone else?"

That was an interesting thought, and it made me wonder if Miranda's racist statements about Marcus were genuine or part of a distraction. If that was the case, though, who was she trying to keep us from seeing? "Do you think she'd do that if her husband killed her dad?"

Mom tilted her head. "Maybe. You'd hope she'd have some loyalty to her father, or at least think about the potential escape that her husband's arrest could mean for her and her girls."

I thought about that as we walked down the lane. "But what if he made her play the witness? What if she didn't have a choice?"

Dad rolled his eyes, but he didn't say anything.

Mom said, "Could be. Worth checking out, don't you think?"

I sighed. It was worth checking out, but the more we talked about this and the further we walked down the driveway of the Harris Ranch, the more guilty I felt. I was clearly breaking my promise to the sheriff, and yet, here I was having this conversation with my parents – the first, non-bickering conversation we'd had in a long time. I sighed and tried to think of other things besides my own guilt.

As we approached Harris's house, I wondered about whether they'd lived here when Miranda was a little girl. I could picture her running around the place, chasing chickens and climbing trees. It seemed like a nice place to grow up, especially if those oil pumpjacks weren't running all the time when she was a kid. With each rotation, they made a series of mechanical clicks and then a whooshing whistle when the derrick rose up again. It wasn't really a bad sound, but I thought it might wear on you after being around it constantly.

"This is some place," Dad said. "What exactly are we looking for?"

I looked around. "I don't really know. I just thought maybe something would become clearer if I came back in. Maybe I missed something the first time I was out here."

"On Monday, you mean," Mom said.

I looked over at her, expecting some snide look, but she was studying the house. "Someone is living there."

"Oh, I don't think so, Mom. Harris was a widower. Miranda's mom died when she was about twelve, Cate said. She didn't have any brothers and sisters, and her dad never remarried. So I expect the house is empty."

"No, definitely not empty. Look at the porch. Someone's been watering the geraniums in the window boxes. See the water on the deck boards?"

Sure enough. There were little puddles under the planter boxes. "Well, Homer may just be watering the flowers, keeping the place nice."

"Homer?" Dad asked.

"The caretaker. He's running the operation until Miranda gets her feet back under her." I told them about running into him the day before at the taco truck.

"That's nice of him. A place like this can't be left untended, that's for sure." Dad whistled as he counted at least seven oil derricks in our view from the front of the house. "Too much temptation."

I nodded and wondered, randomly, how much a barrel of oil weighed.

"I suppose he could just be caring for the flowers, but something about the way that house sits, it feels lived in." Mom was staring at the front windows

I followed her gaze. "What do you mean?"

"I don't know exactly. The house just feels alive, I guess, like someone is opening and closing that screen door regularly." She laughed. "Maybe I'm psychic."

I rolled my eyes this time just as my phone buzzed in my back pocket.

"All set," Stephen's text said.

"Be back in ten," I typed before I turned to Mom and Dad. "Ready to head back?"

"They're done?" Mom asked.

I nodded, and we started back up the driveway. As we walked, I looked out over the land around us. Most of it was just pasture with cattle grazing away, but just up by the road, I saw a golden brown field. I immediately thought of "America The Beautiful" and its "amber waves of grain."

"Winter wheat," Dad said. "I've always loved it because it's this vibrant green all winter and only turns brown like this when everything else is greening up again. Looks about ready to harvest."

I smiled. My dad with all his business background sometimes really surprised me. "It's beautiful."

"Yeah, if you like dead things," Mom said snidely. There was the Mom I knew and loved. I bumped her with my hip, and she giggled.

Dad squeezed my shoulder again and then gave me a gentle shove through the bushes at the end of the road. As we turned onto 33, I heard a car start up behind us and I wondered if Homer had been there. I would have liked to have said hi, be neighborly. After all, he'd just lost a friend, too. At least I expected Harris had been at least a friend of sorts.

MOM AND DAD spent the afternoon in the bookstore reading. Every once in a while, one or the other of them would get up and ask if they could help with anything. But I knew they loved to read – I'd gotten that right down the family tree – so I let them enjoy their books with Mayhem at their feet.

Around six, Daniel stopped by, and Mom asked if the four of us could go to dinner together, their treat. I was not one to pass up a free meal, especially the kind of meal my parents liked, and when Daniel agreed, I led him to a corner and asked him to go pick up a dress from my closet. I needed something other than my jeans and sweater, and I hoped he'd also realize that cover-alls might not work for him either.

Sure enough, when he came back with my dress – and a thin chain from my jewelry box to go with it – he was in khakis and a button-down shirt. This man was amazing. I gave him a quick kiss as I scooted to the back room to change.

I was just about to lock up when Max Davies came in. Daniel was in the café helping Rocky clean-up, and Mom and Dad weren't back from the house yet after they ran home to change and drop off Mayhem and Taco for a canine hangout on the couch. I felt a little exposed in my black sheath dress and heels, and I hoped Daniel would come back quickly. Max didn't scare me or anything, but I didn't love the way he looked at me either – his eyes were just so hopeful.

"Hi Max. We're just closing up. What can I do for you?" I tried to make my voice sound casual while also looking desperately at the café as if I could send Daniel a telepathic message.

"You look lovely," Max said as he bent to take my hand and kiss it. "I'm glad I caught you." He smiled, a sweet by slightly sad smile. "I know I may be very forward in asking this, but I wondered if perhaps some evening I could cook you a special meal for two in the restaurant."

I studied him for a second and said, "Oh, that's very kind, Max. That would be lovely. Thank you." It was only when an arc of sheer delight passed across his face that I realized my mistake. "You mean, a meal for Daniel and me, right?" I stammered.

His delight only faded slightly. "Why would I do that? No, for you and I." His voice was assured, profoundly so.

I tried to keep my face composed, but I could feel my eyes widening. I took a deep breath through my nose and said, "Well, that's very kind, Max. Really. But you know I am dating Daniel, right?"

He nodded, unfazed. "I do, but I figured now was my chance. I think we could be a lovely duet, Harvey. I'd love the opportunity to impress you, perhaps steal you away from that mechanic." He said the word *mechanic* like it was a euphemism for poop.

I wasn't tempted by his offer in the least, but I had considered the kindness of it until his mechanic line. Then, I was done. I could not stand snobbery of any sort, especially not about profession.

I unclenched my jaw and said, "Thank you, Max, but Daniel and I are very happy. I hope you have a good night."

A hand slipped around my waist lightly, and I looked over my right shoulder to see Daniel smiling. "Nice to see you, Max. Have a good night."

Max's face flushed a hue of red akin to a beet, but from embarrassment or anger I couldn't tell. His emotions were made very clear, however, when he smacked the bell above the door and sent it rattling on his way out.

"He took that well, I think," Daniel said with a half-smile. "Thank you. We are very happy." He gave me a soft kiss.

When I pulled back, I looked up at him, "How long were you there?"

"Oh, I saw him come in. He's been asking all around town about our 'status,' so I figured he was up to something. I knew you'd handle it though." He pulled me close.

"I was sending you the telepathic bat signal of help," I said as I looked up at him.

"I'll always be here, Harvey, but rarely will you actually need me. You've got this, all of it, well in hand."

I snuggled my head into his chest and sighed.

inner at the steakhouse in Salisbury with Daniel, Mom, and Dad was surprisingly delightful. It felt like we'd turned a corner, like maybe my parents would be a part of my life in a more significant way.

When we got back to our house, Mom said, "It's such a pretty night. Anyone up for a stroll?" Mayhem and Taco almost took her off her feet in their enthusiasm while we humans slipped on jackets and moved more calmly toward the door. As we walked, we talked about dogs since Mayhem and Taco were particularly insistent on sniffing and tripping us all up by wrapping us in their leashes again and again.

It turned out my parents were looking for a dog. "One that is small and that we can train to travel," Dad said. "And that likes to lie around with other dogs."

At first, I tried to talk them into a cat, pointing out that Aslan was a prime example of the self-sufficiency and lack of neediness that felines provided. I refrained from saying that my parents were really probably not up for a dog. But when Mom began a tirade about cat hair and litter boxes, I gave up that tack on the topic and grinned. "I could see you all with a French Bulldog."

Mom laughed. "They look like giant bats, very cute giant bats. But we were thinking a dog from a local shelter. Maybe one who is a bit older. Is your local shelter open tomorrow?"

I looked at Daniel, and the surprise must have shown on my face because he smiled and said, "I think so. But if not, I know the animal control officer. I can get you in."

"Great. Then in the morning, we're going dog shopping." She furrowed her brow. "Maybe it's not appropriate to say you're shopping for a living thing." She glanced at Dad and gave a firm, single nod of her head. "We're going to get our new family member."

I am pretty sure I walked the rest of the way home with my mouth open. Who was this wonderful woman, and what had she done with my mother?

I WOKE up thinking about my parents as dog owners and settled down my hope, knowing that maybe it had been the wine talking. But when I got up, Mom had made steel cut oatmeal with strawberries, and she and Dad were ready to head out the door to the shelter so that they'd be there at ten, when they opened. I didn't think the animal shelter was quite like a wedding dress sale at an exclusive boutique in New York City, but I didn't want to damper their enthusiasm with tiny bits of reality.

"So you're serious?" I asked between bites of the gooey, delicious oatmeal.

"Yep. It's time we slowed down. Time we took stock of what matters." She put her hand over mine and softened her voice the way she used to when she was about to tell me she and dad were going out of town and leaving me with my very kind, but very old, Aunt Louise. "Your dad and I want to run something by you."

I pulled my hand back. Now, they weren't talking about Aunt Louise anymore, God rest her soul, but this was usually the place in the visit where the conversation about my chosen career came up, and I really didn't want to go there. "Maybe we can just focus on the dog this morning," I said a little more sharply than I intended.

Mom shot Dad a look, and he gave her a quick nod. Something was going on, but I could wait to find out what. It wasn't likely to be good news.

When my parents left to pick out their new pet, Stephen and Walter were still sleeping. They'd gotten in late after a night of celebration in Annapolis. Their offer had been accepted on the house. I was so excited that we were going to be neighbors that I left them a bottle of champagne right next to a fresh jar of orange juice that I squeezed myself.

Then, I finished getting ready and enjoyed the solitary walk into work with Mayhem. She was always a bit more subdued when it was just her and me, so we meandered our way through the streets of town and arrived at the shop just in time to see a silver pick-up pull away.

I ran the last block, hoping against hope that my shop windows weren't broken and that I didn't see fire blazing behind the glass. But everything looked fine. Still, to be cautious, I texted the sheriff to let him know I'd seen the truck again, and he said he'd be over shortly.

I let Daniel know, too, and asked Stephen and Walter to come in when they could. As I was finishing up my texts on the side-walk, Rocky walked up, a plate of cinnamon rolls in her hand, and I let her know what had just happened.

"You haven't gone in yet, right?"

"Nope. I didn't want to go in alone, just in case." I shrugged. "Feels a little silly."

"Not silly at all." She took a hard breath. "Okay, let's go."

I opened the door slowly, thinking of all those movies where bombs were triggered by trip wires and only took a breath again when the door was fully open and all three of us were inside without incident.

That's when I saw the note on the floor, written in magazine letters like some ransom letter. "Stay away from Miranda Harris if you know what's good for you."

Then, I was *very* glad I'd asked the sheriff to come. A threatening note was not something I took lightly.

"What in the world?" Rocky said. "First they threaten you in their car and now they leave a note. Don't threats usually escalate." She gave me a small smile. "I mean at this point, a note is a little anticlimactic, don't you think?"

"Good point. When I find out who is threatening me, I'll remind him that he should be building the tension with his threats." I gave her my most convincing "I'm not terrified" smile and told her I was fine waiting for the sheriff while she got the coffee going. "I'm going to need a very large latte though."

"On it," she said as she and the cinnamon rolls head to the café.

While I waited for Sheriff Mason, I studied the note as it lay on the register counter. I couldn't tell anything about what kind of magazines the letters came from. They looked pretty generic to me. But I did notice that the author called her Miranda Harris, not Miranda Harris-Lewis. I wasn't sure that meant anything, but it was notable.

The sheriff arrived quickly, and I handed him the note that I'd picked up with a tissue. I always felt silly worrying about fingerprints and stuff, but too much TV had made me over-cautious.

He slipped the note into a baggy with a red top – just like on the shows, I noted – and I asked if he could speak to Rocky first since she looked to have her opening process well in hand and I hadn't even started mine. "Totally fine, Harvey."

I checked the floor and set up the register, turned on the neon sign, and just before ten the sheriff took my statement and then went to browse for a few minutes while I opened. We always had a few die-hards waiting to get in on Sunday – mostly for Phoebe Chevalier's cinnamon rolls – and the sheriff was kind enough to try to blend in rather than cause a stir by being at the register, notebook in hand.

After the first customers came in and took to their seats or got their gooey goodness, the sheriff came back. He'd been totally focused on the note – where it was, what I saw about the truck, etc. – when we'd spoken a few minutes before, but now, his notebook was away, and he was giving me a good stare down. "Harvey, have you been snooping?"

"No." I paused. "Not really. I mean it. Mom, Dad, and I were taking a walk yesterday, and we went down the driveway at the Harris place as we walked—"

"Past the locked gate, you mean?" He didn't look happy.

"Yes." I didn't figure there was much reason to say more.

"Harvey, you were trespassing."

I blushed. I hadn't thought of it like that. "You're right. I'm sorry." I seemed to be saying that a lot lately. "I didn't really think of it out that way." I told him how we'd been out to see Stephen and Walter's house and really had just gone for a walk.

"I hear you. I get that it wasn't that you set out to do that, but still, you did it. Your intentions don't really matter."

"Am I in trouble?" I suddenly had images of big fines and being unable to contribute to the mortgage, of losing my store. I had to take deep breaths to keep the panic at bay.

He sighed. "No. Technically, it's abandoned until Miranda decides what to do with it. So no harm done. But no more, Harvey. Stay away from everything to do with this case." He practically wagged a finger in my face.

I nodded. "Sheriff, my mom pointed out something while we were there. I just remembered when you said the place was abandoned. She noticed that someone was watering the flowers on the front porch."

"Hmm. I guess Homer could be doing that, or Miranda, although I'm not sure she has the energy to do much besides grieve and recover just now."

"Something else, too. I think I heard a car start as we were leaving. I didn't see a car, but then I didn't look too hard. Just felt like someone was out there." I thought about what Mom said about the housing feeling lived in. "Does Homer live there?"

The sheriff looked puzzled. "No. He used to, but Miranda asked that he move once her dad died. He goes out to check on the place each day, I think. Maybe it was him. I'll ask."

I nodded. "Cool." I looked down at my Birkenstocks. "I really am sorry."

"I know, Harvey." He met my eyes when I looked up. "You've just got to think first. Take a moment. Make better choices."

I knew he was right. I was really impulsive, and sometimes, that was downright dumb.

He hitched his belt up and said, "If you see this silver truck again, you call me on my cell. No matter what time." He held up the note in the red-lined bag. "This is a serious threat, Harvey. You know that, right?"

I looked again at the note and shivered. "I do. Thanks, Sheriff."

He gave Rocky a wave as he left, and I tried to put the threat out of my mind as I enjoyed my favorite day of the week in the bookstore.

FORTUNATELY, we were slammed, and I didn't have a minute to do much but answer questions, ring up purchases, and tidy shelves until late afternoon. Just this week, Marcus and I had agreed to try and take one weekend day a week off each, so I was covering Sundays, and I would get Saturdays off. But about noon, he came in anyway, saying he just wanted to read. But of course, he couldn't resist helping out, and for once, I didn't shoo him away. He was salaried, so I didn't feel bad for having him work a few hours. But still, I snuck a minute to order him a leather-bound hardcover of *American Pastoral*, a book that was one of his favorites, as a small thanks for all the extra work he did.

Just around six, I looked out and saw Miranda Harris-Lewis and her daughters in the children's section reading a book together. I watched casually until she looked over, and then I waved. She smiled and gave a small wave back. I sauntered over, wanting to be casual but also very much eager to hear how she and the girls were.

As soon as the girls saw me, they jumped up and ambushed my legs with hugs. "Harvey, Harvey, you're here!"

Miranda followed them over. "They were afraid you'd be gone for the day," she said quietly. "They wanted to thank you."

"Yes," one of them said. "Thank you for saving us."

For a moment, I was very puzzled and a bit alarmed that the girls might have thought I had killed their father. My anxiety must have shown on my face because Miranda said quickly, "For saving them on Wednesday when their dad came home early."

"Oh," I said, suddenly feeling both very vulnerable and very humble. "Glad I could help." I tried to smile, but all of this felt very sad.

"Girls, why don't you each go pick out a book? I need to talk to Harvey for a second."

The girls gave each of my thighs another hug and then headed to the picture books.

"Miranda, I don't really know what to say." I looked her in the eyes and tried to communicate both my sadness and relief for her.

She put her hand on my arm and said, "It's okay. I don't either." She sank into the chair behind her. "I'm glad it's over. . . but I'm a widow now, too."

I sat down in the chair beside her and took a deep breath. This woman was an entirely different one than the woman who was here just a few days ago accusing Marcus of murder. "I can't imagine," I said. "Do you all have everything you need? I could arrange a meal train or bring over some frozen dinners."

She gave me a half-smile "Actually, we're enjoying the chance to eat out a lot. We weren't really allowed to do that before." Her eyes fell to her lap. "He just couldn't trust me. I don't know why. He just couldn't, and when I tried to figure out what had happened that made him that way . . ."

I reached over and took her hand. "Sometimes, I guess, the wounds people carry leave them only able to wound other people. Maybe he's at peace now."

She squeezed my fingers. "I hope so. I really do."

We sat in silence for a few moments, but then, she looked over at the girls and smiled again. "Anyway, I wanted to thank you for that quick thinking about the modeling thing for the girls. That really did save us." She met my gaze again. "I explained to the girls that this was just a thing to keep Daddy from getting mad, and they understand. We're just so grateful for your kindness that day."

"Hold on there. I may have made that up on the spot, but I honor my word. I really do want the girls to model for us, if that's okay with you." I'd been thinking about it a lot, about how I wanted to do it for the girls but also how their beautiful faces would really be perfect for our upcoming ad campaign.

"Really?" Her eyes were wide, and she glanced back at her daughters before looking back at me. "Really?"

"Really. I was thinking something with summer reading recommendations. We could have the staff and the girls pick their favorites and do a whole campaign around that. What do you think?"

"I can't believe it. That would be amazing. Thank you!"

"Good. I'll get the details pulled together with Mart, my quasi-marketing manager, and get back to you, if that's okay." I couldn't wait to get the photographer with those two cuties, but I knew I needed to ask a question. "This is going to sound so rude, but can you tell me if there's a trick to telling the girls apart?" I blushed.

"Oh goodness. Thank you for asking. So many people don't even try. Yes, there is. Daisy has her ears pierced. Maisy doesn't."

"Perfect. And really easy, even if Daisy doesn't have earrings in."

Miranda nodded. "Yep, just look for the holes." She looked over at her girls again. "They really are my everything. We have some big changes ahead, but I know life is going to be easier for us now."

I smiled. "Forgive me if I'm being nosy, but what's next? I mean, do you have a plan for what you and the girls are going to do? Not that you need a plan? I mean, you could just—"

She interrupted, thank goodness. "We're going to move back to the farm. Beyond that, I'm not sure. But we need to be in a new place, get away from that house with all those awful memories. I know that much."

"Your dad's house is really nice. I bet the girls will love running around there."

She brightened. "You've been there? It is amazing, huh?"

I suddenly felt a little sheepish. A little impulse in me told me to confess and share that I'd been snooping, but I suppressed that guilty voice, not out of guilt but because I didn't want her to feel responsible for forgiving my bad choices. So I just left the why of how I'd been there out of things for now. "It is amazing."

"And it's home, you know. I think we'll all like it there," Miranda gazed out the window. "but I may take up the oil derricks, ask the men who bought the mineral rights to find a less intrusive way to get the oil. Not sure. I just don't like all the noise they make, and they're pretty ugly, too." I nodded. "I'm not deciding anything right now though, that's what Homer suggested."

"That sounds like good advice to me. No decisions for a while. Just let the status quo ride." That's what people had told me when my marriage had fallen apart. I hadn't heeded that wisdom, and it had turned out great for me. But still, I could see how it might be smarter to not make choices in the midst of a crisis.

Miranda stood and called to the girls, who dutifully put back their books and headed over. "Thanks again, Harvey," she said as she put a soft hand on each of her daughters' heads. "Oh, and I forgot. I heard about that truck that's been harassing you. The sheriff asked me about it when I went to, um, when I stopped by his office earlier. You okay?"

I sighed. "I am. Not thrilled that someone is," I looked at the girls, "trying to make me nervous, but I'm okay. You didn't know the truck did you?"

Miranda shook her head. "My dad used to have an old silver pick-up back when I was a kid, but nothing since. Sorry."

I gave her a quick hug. "No worries. I'm sure the sheriff will get it all sorted." I walked them to the front door. "I'll be in touch about the photo session date soon."

"We're going to do it? We're going to be models," Daisy said as the tiny blue gems sparkled in her ears.

"Are we, Mom?" Maisy shouted.

I knelt down and whispered, "My star models."

They squealed and began talking excitedly about outfits as they left the store. Miranda threw me a smile over her shoulder, and I felt my soul lift. Things were looking up. Definitely looking up.

RIGHT ABOUT CLOSING TIME, Mom and Dad came back to the shop with their new dog. He was the spitting image of that 1980s canine Benji, and I just wanted to bury my face in his scruffy fur. Mom mentioned, though, that he'd a flea bath earlier that day, so I refrained.

They had named their new friend Sidecar, and my first thought was that Mom had named a dog after her favorite drink. But Dad quickly told me that they'd chosen the name – discarding the temporary nomenclature of "Beau" that the shelter had bestowed on him – because Dad thought Mom would look adorable on a scooter with the dog in her sidecar.

I had about a million questions about the scooter, Mom on it, the wisdom of a sidecar, and how a dog can be coaxed to stay in such a mode of transport, but I didn't ask any of them because I couldn't get over how cute the dog was and just wanted to snuggle him.

"He's two or three," Mom said, "and in great health. He's had a full physical and all his shots are up to date. He weighs twenty-three pounds and stands seventeen-and-a-half inches high." I'm not sure my mom knew how much I weighed or how long I was when I was born, but she was clearly smitten with this pup . . . and I couldn't blame her.

"I can't believe you got a dog," I said as I rubbed this little guy's belly for the fifth or sixth time. "But he suits you. I'm not sure I could say how, but he feels like a good fit."

Mom beamed at me. "Oh, good. I'm glad you think so. I think he and Mayhem will be good friends."

I laughed. "Oh yes, our girl here will love having him visit. Aslan, well, I'm not sure the feline queen of the house will agree, but she'll survive."

A look passed between Mom and Dad. "What? What did I say?" I asked.

Dad looked around the store that was almost empty of customers and said, "We have something to ask you, Harvey. It's kind of a big conversation, though, and we don't want to keep you from your work."

I sighed. This couldn't be good, and my tired, overtaxed mind flashed to the worst possibilities: cancer, a divorce, some terrible news about Dad's business. "Are you guys okay? Just tell me that much."

The bell over the door rang, and Daniel and Taco came in. I don't know what my face telegraphed to Daniel, but he rushed over and asked, "Are you okay?"

"Um, I think so. Well, maybe. I'm not sure." I looked at my parents again, and their faces were expectant. I couldn't put this off again. "Can you keep an eye on things for just a minute? My parents have something to tell me."

"Sure. Absolutely. Take your time." He headed right to the register, and my parents and I went into the back room for a little privacy.

I was terrified, but I did my best to look excited, just in case my parents needed me to be strong. "So what's up? You planning on moving to St. Marin's, too?"

My dad's mouth fell open. "How did you know?"

"Wait?! What?!" I sat down heavily on a box of books waiting to be unpacked and tried to get my brain to process what I'd just heard. "Are you serious?" I found myself smiling, even though I wasn't sure what was going on. I felt a little light-headed.

Mom rushed over and hugged me. "So it's okay with you, then? I mean we wouldn't bother you or be in your hair or anything."

I pulled back from Mom's embrace. "You're serious? You're moving here? I'm so confused. What is happening?" I looked around the storeroom as if I might find clarity on the bare sheetrock walls.

Dad cleared his throat. "Harvey, if it's okay with you, we'd like to move to St. Marin's. We don't want to crowd you or make you feel obligated to us in any way. It's just that, well, we love this town." He took a long, deep breath. "But even more, we love you, and we realize we haven't been the most attentive parents to you. We'd like to change that."

My dad rarely said much of anything that wasn't a joke or a bit of intense commentary about the state of the world, but here he was saying what I had most wanted to hear my whole life. They were choosing me.

"We've focused too long on our stuff, Harvey. We want to spend the last years of our lives close to you, trying to make up for the time we threw away." My mom's voice was shaky with emotion, and I could see the plea in her eyes.

I stared at my parents and could not find a single word to say.

Mom and Dad looked at each other and then at me. "But if you don't want us to come, that is totally fine. We don't want to intrude or crowd you." Mom sighed and sat down on a box before patting it to ask me to sit next to her. "We know this is sudden, but when we were here earlier in the week, we both loved the town. It's a good size for us, and it has all the things we've been considering for a place to retire."

I switched to the box next to her, and she scooted closer and slipped her arm around my waist. "But really, it was you, Harvey. You and your shop, the friends you have here, Daniel. You've built an entire live in just a few months, and we were not a part of it."

I started to protest, to tell them that I had never meant to shut them out, but I stopped because the truth was I had shut them out. I had because it was the only way to deal with them not choosing me. Now, though, they were here and choosing me in the biggest way possible.

Mom continued, "So if this is too much, you just say the word. We'll go right back to Baltimore—"

"Please come." My voice was quiet and wobbly, but it was the most heartfelt request I'd made from them in decades. "Please. Please come."

I had no memory of ever seeing my mother cry. Be upset, yes. But never shed tears, so when I saw a single tear slide down her cheek, I couldn't hold back and started to weep. Dad sat beside me, and the three of us cried together for a few moments.

Then, like a bolt of lightning, it hit me. "The dog. Sidecar. He's going to be living here . . . with you . . . in a house . . . here."

Dad rubbed my neck and stood up. "That's the plan," he said as he helped Mom up from the box.

"Wait, does that mean you're actually going to get a scooter?"

"Sure does. A mint-green Vespa. I've always wanted one." Mom's voice was light, playful.

"Your business, though, Dad? And Mom, your volunteer work?" My parents weren't the kind of wealthy elite who attended society gatherings in Baltimore museums or anything, but my dad did have a successful accounting firm and Mom did serve on the board for a local animal welfare organization and coached women about interviews at the YWCA.

"I've sold the business, Harvey. Two of the younger partners made me an offer I couldn't refuse, and your mother," he smiled at her tenderly, "she can do her good works here."

Mom pulled me to stand beside them. "That's right. Plus, I'd like to have some time to help my daughter with her business," she squeezed my hands firmly, "in whatever ways would be helpful."

I let out a sigh of relief when she pulled back on her offer a bit. For a second there, I had been picturing a full redesign of my shop in Laura Ashley fabrics. My mother was all florals and pearls. I was not.

"Well, then, I guess you're all set." I tried to keep the hurt out of my voice. After all, we'd just had the most special moment of my forty-three years, but the fact that they'd been planning on all this, that Dad had sold his business without telling me, that hurt.

But then, I had kind of kept them in the dark about my plans to move back to the East Coast. Clearly, we had some work to do on openness in our family . . . and with them here, that would be all the easier. I decided to try and let my hurt go.

"Does this mean you'll be buying a big waterfront house, too? Maybe you can move in next to Stephen and Walter, and I can come over for dinner at your place and then dessert at theirs." I laughed. "I'll never have to cook again."

Mom snickered. "That would work, but we're not sure yet. We haven't even put our house in Baltimore on the market yet." She took my hand again. "We didn't want to do anything until we'd talked to you."

I squeezed her fingers. "Thanks, Mom." I grabbed them both in a clumsy hug before I mentioned that I needed to get back to work.

"Mind if we hang out and walk you home?" Dad said.

"Sure." I paused as I went to open the storeroom door. "What if we had a big cook-out at our place tonight? Dad, you can be the grill master, and we'll go simple – sausages and grilled veggies. What do you think?"

"Depends. Do you have any more wine from Mart's winery?"

"I'll be sure she brings some home." I smiled as I left them in my storeroom.

I felt a little stunned and fuzzy-headed after all this news. It was good news, at least I was pretty sure it was, but it was all a lot . . .

and after this week . . . I just walked right into Daniel's chest and let him hug me.

"You okay?" he said into my hair.

"Yes, I'm good, I think. I'll catch you up in a bit. For now, could you text everybody and ask them to a barbeque at my house? We have lots of things to celebrate."

He raised an eyebrow, but nodded and got out his phone.

By the time we were closing up the shop, everyone we knew was on the way to our house with side dishes and desserts. Mart was bringing a few bottles of wine, as Mom had requested, and I had enlisted Woody's help in getting enough sausages and buns for us all. It was time for a party.

Our backyard was simple – a lawn, a small patio, a tall wooden fence hung with Edison bulbs that made it all seem more quaint than just a regular backyard – but when all of the people you love in the world are in a space, it always feels magical. Cate and Lucas came with some sort of shrimp spread and crackers that the fish eaters devoured, and Stephen and Walter, riding high from the acceptance of their offer on that gorgeous house, contributed a cheese plate "from that little fromagerie" over in Annapolis. They said it like I made my way to Annapolis to shop every day, but I was grateful. I'd never met a cheese I didn't like.

Marcus and Josie brought green salad with the best dressing I've ever had – tart and sweet. Josie promised me the recipe. Elle made roasted beets, and for the first time, I didn't find the vegetable appalling. Luisa brought homemade enchiladas that the sheriff carried in on a ceramic platter the size of my torso, and Rocky and Phoebe came in with chocolate pecan pie for everyone. Daniel grabbed a case of beer at the corner store as we walked home, and with the wine Mart brought in, we had us a good, good party.

I spent most of the night tucked into a chair in the corner of the yard watching. I'd had a lot of people time this week, and it was nice to just observe and sit back. Daniel, always a little reserved in crowds himself, sat beside me, getting me more wine or cheese as I needed it and then dressing a sausage just the way I liked it when Dad declared them ready.

Mom moved through the crowd with a grace I could never muster. She spoke with everyone, and sometimes, I could hear her explaining their decision to move to town. Mart and Cate both gave me surreptitious glances of mock horror when she told them, but I tried to allay their concerns with a hearty thumbs up and a genuine smile.

I watched Rocky and Marcus flirt casually – a hand on her back as he passed, a quick wink when she caught his eye. I wondered if they'd do a mother introduction and thought about facilitating that until I saw that Josie and Phoebe had taken up their own corner and were laughing to beat the band. Looked like things were great.

Stephen and Walter pulled up chairs by Daniel and me after we had all eaten and told us that their offer – just below asking – had been accepted in minutes, and because both they and the sellers were eager to close, they'd be moving in three weeks. "We're flying out Monday to put our house on the market, but our agent has already had two private offers at full asking. It's going to be fun to watch a bidding war." Stephen had a disturbingly gleeful expression as he talked about the delight of getting more money out of everyone, and I was glad to see that Walter was more interested in finding the right people for their gorgeous house. "Money matters, of course," he said, "but people matter more." Stephen patted his husband's knee as if to say, "Sure. Sure," and I laughed.

About eleven, I could feel the activity of the last few days catching up to me. I kept nodding off in my chair, so I asked

Daniel if he wanted to join me and the dogs for a quick walk around the block. He nodded, and I said, "Let me just tell my mom." I didn't want her looking for me and worrying.

She gave me an all-too-knowing smile and winked as Daniel opened the back gate, and we slipped onto the street beside our house. "My mom really likes you," I said as we rounded the corner and headed toward the river.

"I like her, too. Especially now that it seems things are better between you two." He paused then said, "They are better, right?"

I smiled. "Yes, better. Not perfect. That's going to take some time. But better. Definitely better." We walked a few steps, and then I said, "But you handled her, well, her and I, very well. I always need to know you're on my side, but I also need you to love my mom."

"I can love people and still know they do crappy things. And I will always, always be on your side. Always." He bent down and kissed me on the cheek.

I felt tears welling again and decided I needed to lighten the mood. "You met Sidecar, right?"

"You mean the dog that looks freakishly like Benji? Yep, I met him. Does your mother really intend to make that dog ride around with her on a scooter?"

"Yes, I do believe she does. But if that's happening, you better believe I'm taking advantage of that for some advertising. I'll get an ad for the shop to put on Sidecar's, er, sidecar, and offer people five percent off their purchase if they can tell me where they spotted that pair."

Daniel guffawed. "That is perfect, Harvey, and you know, I think your mother might love that idea."

"I think she just might." I whistled. "What in the world is happening?"

Just then, I heard a car engine coming toward us and stepped instinctively away from the road, pulling Mayhem with me. Daniel always walked on the roadside of the sidewalk, a tiny bit of chivalry that made me feel safe. As the car got closer, the lights got brighter, and all the sudden, Daniel shoved hard away from the road with his body, dragging Taco behind him like an anchor.

The silver pick-up missed us by inches.

I sat up on the sidewalk and dug my phone quickly out of my pocket and commanded the operating system to call Sheriff Tucker. We were only on the backside of our block, so he was there in seconds. "That way." I pointed up the street. "He turned left at the next block."

The sheriff had his phone out already. "Harriet, tell everyone to be on the look-out for a silver pick-up." He looked down at Daniel.

"A 73 Chevy C-10 with dual exhaust."

I looked at Daniel as the sheriff relayed the make and model. "You got all that so quickly?"

He rubbed his left shoulder where he'd slammed into the pavement. "It's just instinctual. I see a vehicle, and I automatically ID the kind it is. You do the same with books, right? Someone mentions a title, and you immediately think of the author."

"Yeah, I guess so. But wow, Daniel, thank you." I helped him off the pavement and checked on the dogs. Mayhem was fine, a little scared but fine. Taco, however, wouldn't get up. Daniel tugged his leash and nothing. I knelt down beside the Basset, afraid that he might have gotten hit . . . only to see his tail wagging. He'd gotten an extra chance to lie down, and he'd taken it. "Taco, you are ridiculous," I groaned as I hefted his giant body off the ground.

We all walked back to the house, where everyone was waiting for us after having seen the sheriff sprint out the back gate. I told everyone what had happened and watched all the color fade out of my mom's face.

"We're okay, Mom."

She pulled me to her and then grabbed Daniel with her other arm. "This has to end," she whispered to me. "Tomorrow, you and I go sleuthing."

THE NEXT MORNING I woke with a start to find my mother standing over me. That alone was a surprise, but when my eyes finally focused and I saw that she was dressed completely in black with a knit cap on her perfectly styled hair, I closed my eyes and tried to go back to sleep and pretend this was a dream.

No such luck. Mom was up and ready to "look for clues" as she said, and I had to really restrain myself from saying, "Get a clue, Mom." Instead, I sat up, forced a smile, and said, "Okay, give me a minute to get dressed."

My hope was that when I came out in my usual jeans and a blouse, she'd take the hint and adjust her outfit, but no such luck. When it was time for us to go – an hour earlier than usual for our apparent "sleuthing escapade" – she was still dressed like a diamond thief from a 1940s classic film.

I decided I needed to pick my battles, and since I was already breaking my word to the sheriff, Daniel, and Mart in order to get a little mother-daughter bonding time in, I wasn't sure that my mother's sleuthing attire was the best use of my energy. I needed to reserve my strength to talk her out of this expedition at all.

Mom wanted to drive, insisting we'd need a getaway car that wasn't as easily recognizable as my bumper-stickered Subaru. As I climbed into the passenger seat to try and explain why I couldn't go sleuthing with her, I was trying to find the right words. I gazed out the window down the street to gather my thoughts when the silver pick-up that had been stalking us pulled out from the curb just up my street. They had been watching us.

I shivered, decided to not scare my mom with the news, and convinced myself that Mom was right – this had to stop – all in the time it took Mom to back out of my driveway. This person was determined to terrify me, and I was determined that they would not. Mom and I were going sleuthing.

I pointed up in the direction the truck had just gone and told Mom to head that way. "I have an idea," I said.

"Ooh, this is so fun," she squealed as she, quite literally, peeled out in her Volvo station wagon. Despite my brief desire for vigilante justice, I was regretting my decision to go along with this escapade by the time we reached the edge of town. I found myself kind of hoping that Marcus would call in sick so I'd have an excuse to go into the store and, thus, avoid hurting my mom's feelings *and* breaking my promise – again – to my friends.. Alas, from his texts about setting up a new front table display for a National Mental Health Awareness month, Marcus seemed to be quite well and managing the store just fine without me.

As we cruised south on 33, Mom asked me again about clues, and I said with a fair amount of exasperation in my voice, "This isn't the *Pink Panther*, Mom. We probably aren't going to find a torn receipt or a misplaced hair to lead us to the killer."

She rolled her eyes as she punched the gas and left the town limits. "Of course not. When Jessica Fletcher solves a murder, it's always about a confrontation. We're going to find out who is stalking you and give them a good talking to."

I started giggling at the idea of my mother, in her current attire, confronting a potential murderer. She'd lecture them into a confession. I could see it – her finger in front of their face, her precise pronunciation and discussion of morals, her appeal to their human dignity – and the vision absolutely cracked me up. I couldn't stop laughing, and I doubled over in the passenger seat as my stomach ached.

Mom asked, "What is so funny?" and that set me off even harder. Eventually, I had to roll down the window and gulp in cool air just to get my breath.

"Harvey, really, what is going on? We are trying to figure out who is threatening you, and you are over there cackling like a witch at her cauldron."

I almost let my mind slide back to a vision of my mother in her black stocking cap with her reading glasses around her neck, but I stopped myself before I got going again. I took a few deep breaths and said, "Mom, we're not confronting anyone. In fact, I'm not even sure what we're doing."

Mom looked at me out of the corner of her eye and then put on her turn signal and pulled off the road. "Well, you pointed this way, so I thought we were coming here again."

I looked ahead of us to see the gates of the Harris farm. "What?! No. I was just—" Again, omitting the truth was getting me in trouble. "I told us to go this way because I saw that silver pick-up back at the house, and it headed this direction."

"What?! That truck was at your house again. The nerve." She paused and squinted through the driveway. "Good instincts because isn't that it pulling into that shed thing."

I peered through the bars on the massive gate, and sure enough, that Chevy C-10 was just sliding into the wagon shed beside the house. "I'll be—"

"Harvey Beckett, watch your language." My mother could lie her way out of every parking ticket, weasel a bargain out of an unexpecting sales person, and convince the stodgiest millionaire to donate to the children's hospital, but she could not tolerate swearing. It was crass and uncultured, in her opinion. In fact, her staunch position on this issue was so engrained in me that I almost never swore simply because I hadn't practiced enough when I was young. The words always felt forced, performative, when I said them.

"I was going to say, 'gobsmacked,' Mom," I lied. It had felt like an appropriate time for a mild swear, but this was a battle for another day.

"We have to go see who was driving." Mom was out the door and through the gate before I could even answer.

"Mom," I whisper-shouted, but it did no good. She was off and slinking her way along a culvert beside the driveway. Blind goats could see her from the other side of the highway in her outfit, but she seemed to be having fun . . . and I figured if we were quiet enough we might just be able to get the license plate off the truck and give it to Sheriff Tucker. I winced as I remembered I'd promised him, just the day before, that I'd text him if I even saw the truck again.

We eased our way along the driveway until we were just a few hundred feet from the shed. "This way," I hissed and pointed into the field of winter wheat. "We can sneak around the back, just in case whoever it is went in the house or is in one of the other buildings. No windows on this side." The wheat came up to our waists and was scratchy. The smell reminded me of a box of cereal, and I suddenly realized I hadn't eaten breakfast. I was seriously craving Honey Nut Cheerios.

Mom dropped to her hands and knees, and I stopped to watch her crawl through the field. I had never in my life seen my mother crawl, not even to pick up toys or rescue something from under the sofa. So this was a sight, and I had to resist the urge to take a picture for blackmail purposes later.

I was not about to crawl, so I just bent at the waist to keep low, and we made our way around the small garage-sized building to the far side. There, we plastered ourselves against the back wall and took a breath.

"I'm going to go in. You stay here," I said directly in my mother's ear.

She swatted me away. "No way. We do this together." She had this glint in her eye that made me think she might say something about a mother-daughter duo, so I got moving.

I peered in the window around the far side of the barn and saw the truck inside. I couldn't make out the license plate, so I crept to the front of the building and made sure no one was nearby.

I didn't see anyone, so I waved Mom around, and we slid open the old, swinging door and slipped inside. The windows were really grimy, so all the light was a little dim. But I got down close and copied down the license plate number from the antique tag. Mom snapped a photo, too, which, I had to admit, was a pretty smart idea, and texted it to Dad with a note that said, "I'll explain later. Just keep this handy."

We slid back out the front door and around to the side closest to the road. The jog across the small strip of lawn to the wheat field was easy, and I was feeling pretty confident when we got back into the wheat. I thought it was probably our best bet to stay partially under cover, even though Mom's black outfit probably made it look like a small bear was in the wheat field. I'm not sure my red poppy blouse was much better. But at least we weren't out in the wide open.

About halfway back to the road, I thought I heard an engine and assumed it was a tractor trailer going back out on 33. We kept walking, but soon it became clear that the sound was getting louder and much, much closer. A few more feet, and we saw it – a huge tractor coming our way through the field.

At first, I thought that they must have just been planning to get up the wheat today. I didn't know much about farming, but I remembered what Dad had said about this field being ready to harvest so it made sense that a tractor would be in the field . . . until I realized the machine was cutting right through the middle of the wheat, and even I knew that made no sense. Someone harvesting would be moving through the field systematically. This tractor was aiming right for us.

Mom looked at me, and I saw not the slightest flicker of fear. Instead, board chair Sharon came to life and took my hand. "Run!" she said, and we took off as fast as we could. For a brief moment, I felt like I was in one of those horror movies where the unidentified thing is chasing the helpless victims through a field and was grateful at least I knew it was a tractor. But then, it hit me that it was gaining on us.

Mom tugged my arm hard, leading us to the driveway. I picked up speed, and she did, too, and just before the combine's blades reached our legs, we hit the driveway and broke into a dead sprint for the gate, about twenty feet away. We would have reached it, too, if I hadn't made the classic chase-scene mistake. I looked back, and when I did, I tripped. Mom came back to help me up, and the last thing I saw was a pair of work boots jump out of the tractor cab.

11

I woke up with a blazing headache and groaned. Immediately, I felt a hand on my forehead. "Thank goodness, Harvey. You gave me quite the scare."

"Mom? You're okay?" I tried to sit up but the flash of pain from my forehead sent me back down to the floor.

"Of course I'm okay. He didn't hit me in the head with a shovel."

"I got hit with a shovel? I don't remember that." I reached up and felt the knot at the back of my head.

"You wouldn't, I expect." She laid her cool hands on my neck. "Just lie still. Here, put your head in my lap." She slid her thigh up under my head, and I turned so that my cheek rested against her leg.

"Where are we?" I asked as I tried to look around from where I was lying.

"That building where he put the truck." I could just make out its outline in front of me. "He brought us here. Told me if I didn't cooperate he'd do more than clobber you."

"Who, Mom?"

"I don't know. Some fellow with a beard. Guess when he didn't get us with the combine, he thought maybe kidnapping was better after all."

My head hurt so badly that I couldn't think very well, but something wiggled around by my jaw. "You said a beard?"

"Yeah, kind of long. Youngish guy, maybe thirties. Clearly knew his way around here because he took us right in and put some kind of bar on the door. I've been trying to get out for thirty minutes."

I tried to get my eyes to focus. "I was out for thirty minutes. Wait, how do you know that?"

She held up her phone. "No signal though."

I took a long, deep breath. "Homer."

"What?" Mom leaned down over me. "What did you say?"

"It was Homer. The caretaker here. He's the one."

She let out a long breath and then rubbed my cheek. "Don't think about that now. We just need to find a way to get out of here."

I wasn't thankful for this situation, but if you had to be suffering from a concussion on a dirt floor while being held hostage, it was kind of nice to have your mom around. I said a silent word of gratitude for that tiny gift and put her hand over mine on my cheek.

My head hurt too badly for me to sit up, so I tried to feel around me with my left hand. Just dirt.

I looked around a little. "I saw some old pieces of chain," my mother said. "Old hoe heads, I think. Nothing very useful as a weapon though."

I marveled for just a moment that my mother could identify a gardening implement and then tried to ponder other things. "Obviously, you tried the door."

She gave my face a very light tap. "Obviously. Something is propped against it. Something very heavy." She adjusted my head as she shifted her leg. "Maybe we could dig out."

I clawed at the ground again. Under the top layer, it felt pretty packed, but that was worth a try. "Okay. But maybe we should start with the windows." They hadn't looked very big, but Mom was pretty small. "Let's break one and see if I can boost you out."

"I don't know, Harvey. I think you need to stay lying down."

I sat up and felt like my head was splitting open, but I was able to stay upright. Standing made me feel like I would vomit, but at least I could stand. "I'm okay. I don't think I can run, though. You're going to have to go for help."

In the dim light, I could see my mother studying my face. The composed visage she'd put together as we began this adventure had faded. Now, I just saw the face of a woman who was worried and determined. "Okay," she said with finality.

I studied the window a moment and then threw a rock Mom found in the corner through the window on the road-side of the building. We waited a few minutes, and when we didn't hear anything, I crouched back down on my hands. "Up you go," I said.

Mom leaned over and kissed my cheek before she stepped onto my back, cleared the fragments of broken glass, and went out the window. "I'll be back as soon as I can," she whispered back up to me. Then, she was gone.

I collapsed back into the dirt, my head careening with pain, and waited. I checked my own cell phone only to see that it had charge but no signal, just like Mom's. I did think to check Wi-Fi then, hoping maybe out here someone still had neglected to put a password on their home system, but the signal for "Harris Ranch" was private. I didn't have the mental fortitude to try combinations beyond the obvious "Huckabee," "Miranda," and various versions of "Maisy/Daisy." Nothing worked.

I composed a text to Daniel, then, figuring he was the person I most wanted to talk to right then. I didn't get super mushy – that wasn't our way. But I told him I was so grateful for the way he cared for me and respected me, that I was looking forward to spending a lot of time with him in the future. Then, I saved it as a note marked "For Daniel" and wrote similar sentiments to Mart, Stephen and Walter, and finally my parents, letting them know that I wanted Marcus and Rocky to get ownership of the shop should I not make it.

I don't know why I felt so certain I wouldn't get out of there. Maybe it was the head injury. Maybe just the fact that Homer had been staid enough to kill two people and then stalk me for days. Maybe it simply felt like I was getting everything I wanted in life, finally, and now the universe was going to rip it away.

Whatever the cause, I was sad, but content. My life was great, and if it ended now, so be it.

But that didn't mean I was giving up. I knew there was no way I could get out that window – both because I couldn't reach that high on my own, but also because my hips were not going through that narrow hole. So I started to dig with one of the hoe heads.

I hadn't gotten far, though, when I heard an engine start just outside the door and watched a crack of light appear at the front of the building. A few seconds later, the engine cut off, and Homer Sloan stood in the doorway. I stepped back into the shadows, hoping to buy Mom a few more moments before he noticed she was gone.

"You two okay in here?" He smiled. "Relatively speaking, I mean."

I shrank back further into the shadows. "Homer, what are you doing?"

"For all that sleuthing, it sure took you long enough to figure out it was me." His voice was like acid. "You are really pretty stupid."

I couldn't really disagree, given my circumstances, but his insults were quickening my heartrate and helping me manage the pain in my head. "Maybe. But why? Did Huckabee do something to you or what?"

His cracking laugh bounced off the wooden walls. "That man was ridiculous. A joke. He couldn't do what needed to be done." He took a step further into the building.

I tried to make myself look bigger while thinking, *Run, Mom, Run!* "So what did you think he needed to do? Did you want a raise or something?" I knew that goading him wasn't probably my best bet, but I had to buy time somehow.

"You think this is about money. You're just like him. I don't care about money. I only care about her."

Revelation struck like a hammer against the inside of my skull. "Miranda!"

"Ding, ding, ding." He came into the room. He had something in his hand but I couldn't make out what. "That monster beat her bloody almost every day, and her father didn't do anything. He was too afraid. His only solution was to send her and the girls away, try to get them to go to Boston and hide, and I couldn't have that. She needed to be with me."

"You killed Huckabee Harris because he was trying to protect his daughter?"

"You think that's protection. Making her go on the run, leave everything she knew behind? That's not protecting her. He wanted to protect himself, protect his legacy."

I wasn't following completely. "His legacy? You mean his money?"

He took another step forward, and I saw that he was carrying a pickax. "His legacy, the inheritance he was leaving those girls."

Now, I was genuinely confused. "I'm sorry. Help me understand, Homer. You killed him because he wanted to leave money to his granddaughters."

He tossed the ax up on his shoulder, and I tried to hide part of my body behind the front of the truck, hoping he'd think Mom was beside me still.

"I killed him because he didn't do what a good father should have done."

"You wanted him to kill Rafe. Is that it? And he wouldn't do it because he was afraid they'd seize his assets and the girls wouldn't get anything? Am I following now?"

Homer stopped and sighed. "Yes. Now you're getting it. He was more worried about what people would think of him than of saving his daughter. Now, isn't that ridiculous?"

I didn't really think avoiding murder at all costs was ridiculous, but I could see a certain form of logic in what he was saying. Twisted logic, but if he . . . "You loved her?"

"Of course I loved her. I've loved her since high school."

Miranda Harris. That's why he'd used her maiden name – he'd

known her longest that way. I almost felt bad for the guy. Almost. "And she never was interested."

"She's not like that. Don't make her sound all haughty and stuff. That's not the real her. She just loved me like a brother, she said. I simply hadn't found the right way to woo her yet. Now, though—"

"*Now*, you think that since you've killed her father and her husband she'll know just how lucky she is to have your love." My voice was oozing with sarcasm, but apparently, Homer was not a whiz at reading tone.

"Exactly. I saved her. She has to love me now." He looked back over his shoulder for a minute like he'd heard something, but then turned back to me. "Your mom is really quiet back there. She didn't strike me as the type of person who would let you take all the limelight."

Now he was a master of observation? "So what's your plan, Homer?" I had to distract him. "How are you going to tell Miranda about your grand gesture?"

He paused and looked toward the window, the window I had broken. "Well, I thought I could offer to take her and the girls to dinner—" He ran over to the window. "You broke the window?!" Then he sprinted over to me and looked all around. "Where's your mom?"

"How did you know she was my mom anyway?"

"Where is she?"

"She went to get help. They'll be here any minute."

He grabbed my arm and began dragging me forward, the pickax swinging from his other arm. "Well, she'll be too—"

A resounding clang sounded through the building, and I fell backwards onto my butt as the sound reverberated in my aching head. When I looked up, there was my mom, shovel in hand, standing over Homer's prone body.

"Come on, Harvey. We have to move." I scrambled to my feet and tried to run for the door. My head hurt so badly, though, that the best I could do was a rough stumble. We made it outside, and Mom slammed the shovel handle against the door. "Run, Harvey."

I followed her down the driveway as quickly as I could. "Mom, is help coming?"

"I don't know. I couldn't leave you. I was almost to the road when I saw him come back, and I just couldn't leave you alone."

"You came back for me? Mom, you shouldn't have." I was speaking the truth, but I was also so happy, even though a love-sick murderer was about to kill us. My mom had come back for me.

"I'm your mother, Harvey. What was I supposed to do?"

I grabbed my head as a wave of pain and nausea washed over me.

Mom slid her shoulder under my arm and helped me pick up the pace just as we heard an engine come to life in the barn behind us.

"You have to run, Harvey," and we did. As fast as we could right back into that wheat.

Clearly Homer was not precious about his truck – Huckabee's truck, because I suspected this was the one Miranda remembered – because he careened right after us, sliding that truck into a low gear and plowing right into the wheat.

I remembered something about zigzagging to avoid capture and told Mom. "We're not dodging bullets, Harvey. Just run straight for the road."

He was gaining on us, though. I could hear it . . . but then I heard another sound, a gunshot. Then voices.

The engine cut off, and Mom and I collapsed into the wheat just as Dad and Daniel ran up. "Where did you come from?"

"I got your text," Dad said to Mom.

"And I got yours," Daniel added. If I hadn't already felt so nauseated, I certainly would have then. I hadn't meant to send that. In fact, I thought I had been in my Notes on my phone, not the messages. Gah!

"Oh," was all I could say.

Daniel bent down and wrapped his arms around me, pulling me to my feet as he whispered. "I want to spend a lot more of my days with you, too, Harvey."

This would have been the spot in a romance novel where we kissed, but given my nausea, I held back for another time. "Where's Homer?"

"The sheriff has him," Dad said with a wave over his shoulder toward the truck. "He's being arrested as we speak."

I turned slowly – my head spinning – and saw the sheriff leading Homer back to his patrol car. "Looks like he's got this under control. Let's go." I really, really wanted to avoid a conversation with the sheriff, especially when my head felt like a small creature was trying to burrow out from behind my right eye socket. "Come on." I started toward the car.

But Dad put a hand on my arm. "The sheriff is on his way over, Harvey. He needs your statement."

I looked at my mom, and she shrugged. I'd definitely seen her feet moving toward the car, too.

"We're here, Harvey." Daniel wrapped his arm around my waist. "You're not alone."

I took a deep breath. He was right. I wasn't. I smiled, felt the shrew in my brain dig in further, and leaned hard against Daniel. "Let's get this over with."

The sheriff's face was a hard plane when he walked over. "Harvey, Sharon," he took a deep breath and then his voice boomed across the field, "what on God's green earth were you thinking?"

I could tell in the set of Mom's shoulders that she had just shifted into "take no prisoners" mode. "What was I thinking? I was thinking that someone was threatening my daughter, and no one was doing anything about it. That's what I was thinking." Her voice was quiet but cutting, like a thin sheet of ice.

Dad put a hand on her shoulder as if to say, "Ease back, Sharon."

"I was doing something, Sharon," the sheriff said through clenched teeth. Then, he let out a long breath. "But if my daughter was threatened, I could be fierce to protect her, too."

Mom gave a curt nod and looked away. I was pretty sure I saw tears in her eyes.

"But Harvey, you gave me your word, and you almost died. That blow to the head alone . . ." He stopped, took another long breath, and said, "But you're okay. You're okay."

I looked at him closely. He wasn't the kind of man who would cry in this sort of circumstance, but I could see the quiver in his jaw. Oh, I felt terrible, and not just from the shovel to the head. "I'm sorry, Tuck. I really am." I wanted to explain how I'd gotten caught up in the excitement of doing something with my mom, how I didn't want to disappoint her. But I didn't want to make her feel bad or responsible for something that was my choice, so I stayed quiet.

The sheriff put a hand to my throbbing cheek. "I need your statements, but first, an ambulance is in order. I'll get your statement now, Sharon, over here." He pointed back toward the house. "Harvey, I'll get yours at the hospital."

I tried to protest, tried to say I was fine, but given that my vision was now doubling and my nausea increasing, I figured I probably needed to get some attention. "Okay," I said as I dropped to the ground among the wheat again. "I'll just wait here."

12

By the time the doctors were done scanning and palpating me – that expression always sent my skin crawling – I was thoroughly exhausted and even more thoroughly ready to go home. Fortunately, despite my parents' intense pressure on the doctor to the contrary, she released me to bed rest.

Daniel offered to give me a ride home, and by the time we got back into town, I'd convinced him that I would recover better at the bookstore. "After all, I'll just worry about it if I'm not there. Better for me to see what's going on, right?"

Bless the man's heart, he must have figured arguing about this was worse for me than giving in because we stopped at home where I changed into yoga pants, my favorite "Got Books?" T-shirt, and a Salisbury U sweatshirt and then went to the store.

Marcus must have been forewarned because when I arrived, a wingback chair had been pulled up by the register, and he had added a small table, a cup of tea, and a very soft, sugar cookie. I was especially grateful for the cookie because I was famished, but eating felt like chewing glass. At least this glass was sweet.

I took up my position with a low stool under my feet and proceeded to greet my "adoring public" as Mom described them. She and Dad had gone to my house after giving an official statement at the police station, changed and come right to the store to help Marcus out while Daniel gave Mayhem and Taco a stroll. Mom greeted everyone who came in and handed them the cards I'd recently had printed up to tell people we could order almost any book they wanted before suggesting that they stop over and say hello to their "hometown hero."

I was less than thrilled with this moniker, but I didn't have the will or the energy to argue. Besides, we were already getting some special orders from her efforts, perhaps driven by a fear of disappointing such an enthusiastic greeter. She was going to be great as part of Mart's PR team.

Since I was on strict orders from the doctor and everyone I knew to not move around a lot and to rest as much as possible, I was funneled all the book recommendation requests. Someone wanted a great book of essays, and I recommended Jo Ann Beard's *The Boys Of My Youth*. A young girl got up the nerve to ask me, with a good bit of encouragement from her dad, what my favorite picture book was, and I had to recommend *Piggies* by Audrey Wood. But by far, my favorite request was from a quiet young woman in her twenties. She wanted to read something that would make her feel "all the things," she said. I asked her for a few minutes to consider, and she headed to the café for a cup of coffee.

I pondered that request hard. I'd been feeling a lot the past few days – forgiveness, excitement, terror – and I didn't think I could come up with a book that could carry that much of the human experience within it. But then, I thought of Uwem Akpan's *Say You're One Of Them*, a collection of short stories by a Nigerian priest that had left me profoundly optimistic about our hope as human beings while still bringing me to tears at the tragedy of what we, as people, do to one another. When the young woman came back, I placed the book in her hands after asking Marcus if he'd grab a copy for me, and said, "This book will change you." She smiled and thanked me as she headed to check out.

I took a deep breath. I was reminded that this was the best part of my job, this opportunity to share the stories I loved so much. Plus, sitting this way, I felt a bit like a legendary wise woman dispensing insight from her throne. I could get used to this.

As the day came to a close and the customer stream got thinner, I sat back and closed my eyes. I thought about Homer, about the way love had driven him to murder, and I thought about Miranda, about the way love had driven her to victimhood. I even considered Rafe, the way that maybe, somehow, his mistaken sense of love for Miranda had led him to control her. I wasn't willing to grant, though, that he had been acting out of love. No, only something very broken makes someone act that way.

I opened my eyes and looked over at my parents as they helped Rocky wipe down tables and empty coffee carafes. Sometimes love just takes a while to flesh out, I realized.

At that moment, the bell over the shop door rang, and I smiled to see Daniel returning with Mayhem and Taco. He'd taken them out to the beach to run for a while, hoping that would mean they'd both sleep really well tonight. He pulled the stool out from behind the counter and sat down next to me. I was very glad to see him, and I also dreaded this conversation.

"The dogs look plum tuckered," I said as I watched them collapse, side by side, in the large bed in the front window.

"Oh yeah, they ran hard. Those commercials with Basset Hounds on the beach lie. There is no grace in that combination."

I laughed and then winced. My head was still throbbing.

"Still hurting, huh? Did the meds help?"

The doctor had given me a prescription for some really high dose painkiller that Mom had insisted on getting filled and then practically shoving down my throat.

"Yeah, they do. But they may be wearing off." I took a deep breath. "Which means I should probably say this before you wonder if the Percocet is talking."

"Harvey, we don't have to do this now."

I smiled at him. "Daniel, you know I don't do well with putting things off. I'm kind of – what's the nice way of saying it? – spontaneous."

"You can say that again." He looked me in the eyes. "I liked the text, Harvey. A lot."

"Well, I'm glad to hear that. I meant every word," I broke eye contact and looked at my hands, "even if I might not have been quite ready to say all that in person."

He took my hands. "I get it. Written words are your thing, but I'm glad you said those things," he gripped my hands tighter, "because I've been wanting to say something and just needed the right time."

I felt my heart kick up a notch and glanced around, sure that my mother or Marcus or someone would interrupt. But oddly, we were completely alone.

"I love you, Harvey Beckett." He smiled and pulled my hands to his chest. "And if you ever scare me like that again . . ." His voice drifted off, too overcome with emotion to finish the statement.

"I'm so sorry, Daniel. I never meant for any of this to happen." I looked down, but then realized I was about to do that thing that people on TV shows do and forget to actually say *it* back. I was going to mess all this up, so I took a breath, looked up into his eyes, and said, "I love you, too."

He put a hand gently to my chin and kissed me. And of course, then, everyone in the store cheered. Talk about embarrassing, but I didn't really care. We were in love.

I had just begun the very slow process of getting out of my chair when Mart, Stephen, and Walter rushed in with looks of deep concern on their faces. They'd been down in the mountains of Virginia wine-tasting and hadn't had any cell signal for most of the day. But as soon as they got Daniel's message about my injury, they rushed home, driving the back roads to avoid the wild and wooly traffic around DC.

"Harvey?!" Mart rushed over, dropped to her knees, and put her hand to my jaw, avoiding the swelling I could feel on my temple. "Woman! You are made of steel."

"Not hardly," I said as I winced. "I feel like I've been kicked in the head by a donkey."

"That's not far off," Daniel said. "Homer is a sort of an a—"

Stephen interrupted by holding up a bag of peas. "My mother always swore by frozen peas as the cure-all for bumps and bruises." He wrapped the bag in a dishcloth Mart had grabbed from the café and gently pressed it to my face.

I winced again, but smiled, too. "Thank you. I'm sure it will help."

Walter sat down on the floor beside where Stephen knelt and said, "We need to hear the whole story, of course, but given how it looks like you feel – no offense," he gave me a small smile, "maybe we'd better wait until everyone else gets here."

"Everyone else?" Mom said. "I don't know that Harvey is up for a performance." She placed her hand on my shoulder and stood like a sentry behind the chair.

I placed my hand over hers and smiled. "Who is coming?"

Mart dropped back to the floor and sat beside Stephen. "Cate and Lucas, Woody, Elle, Tuck and Lu, even Max wanted to come by." She gave me a knowing look, and I rolled my eyes and found out that even the edges of my eyes ached. "We're having a picnic, Mama Sharon. Nothing fancy. Everyone just wants to be sure Harvey is okay. We won't stay long."

As if on cue, my friends came in one after the other, each bearing a plate full of food that was perfect for sitting on the floor. Rocky and Marcus brought over paper plates and cups for the lemonade that Elle brought in. Cate spread out two plaid blankets and then placed platters of cheese, crackers, and fruit at the center. Max contributed the fried mushrooms that I loved so much, and Woody lay two long sausages and a cutting board next to Daniel. "Venison sausage."

I tried not to grimace. I never could get around the idea of eating Bambi. I didn't think I could chew sausage anyway. Still, I was grateful he was here.

Daniel and Mom were whispering behind me, and while I couldn't hear all of what they were saying, I got the idea that Daniel was gently but clearly telling my mom that this is what I wanted and that I would appreciate the company. He was right. After a week as trying as I'd had, it felt amazing to have friends, good friends, nearby.

Max took a seat right next to my chair, his shoulder against my shin, and I stared wide-eyed at Mart until Mayhem, not a girl to miss a snack, pushed between Max and me and stood ready for any morsels that fell. I reached down with a hand and scratched her ear, "Good girl," I whispered.

We ate in silence for a while, and then, finally, Cate said, "I know you don't want to talk much, Harvey, but we'd really like to know what happened."

I looked over at the sheriff, and he gave me a nod. "I'll fill in the details if things seem sketchy. Nothing to keep back, though, since we have our man. You can tell anyone anything you'd like." He still didn't looked thrilled with me, but I appreciated his presence nonetheless.

"First, let me ask," Stephen said, "did this happen because you were sleuthing? I need to know if I must suppress a lecture tonight."

I sighed. "Yes, I was sleuthing, and yes, please no lectures tonight." I placed a hand against my cheek. "I think I've learned my lesson."

"I doubt it," I heard Mart say under her breath as she winked at me.

I told them about following the truck and wanting to just take a look around at the Harris place. Mom filled in the details like she was the soundtrack for a movie thriller, and when she told them how Homer had clocked me with the shovel, everyone winced. I had to admit, we made a pretty good storytelling team, if not the best detectives in the world.

By the time we got to the part where Daniel and Dad showed up, everyone was sitting forward with deep looks of concern on their faces. I was growing tired, and reliving the day's events was more emotionally taxing than I'd imagined it would be. So I asked the sheriff to finish the story of Homer's arrest and the next steps.

"He'll be arraigned tomorrow, and then I expect he might take a plea since he was caught dead to rights, no pun intended."

"So he confessed to both Huckabee's and Rafe's murders?" Woody asked.

"He did," the sheriff replied. "It was weird. He was proud of it, acting like he'd done a good thing. Apparently, it was easy for him to get the poison into Huckabee's gum since he was in and out of the farmhouse all the time, and Rafe kept a pretty regular routine of jogging on 33 after work each night. I expect when we check the truck, we'll find evidence of the hit and run, not that we need it."

Max reached over Mayhem and put his hand on my knee. "I'm so glad you're okay, dear Harvey."

Daniel reached down, took Max's hand off my knee, and helped me to my feet. "So am I." Then he leaned over and kissed me in public for the second time that day. He was a kind, gentle man, my Daniel, but I was also his, and he needed Max to know that.

I grinned at Daniel and snuck a peek at Max, who looked not one bit put off or disappointed by Daniel's declaration, and I sighed. I wondered what it would take for him to get the hint.

I looked at my friends, all seated at my feet, and smiled. "Thank you all for being here. This was exactly what I needed. But now, I need to go home, find a certain fat cat, and watch a movie that doesn't involve shovels, combines, or silver trucks." Daniel wrapped his arm around my waist and led me to the door. "Marcus, you'll close up?"

"You got it, Ms. B. And I'm opening tomorrow. You rest."

I smiled. "Thank you." Thank goodness for Marcus.

Mom and Dad drove Daniel and me to my house with Mart, Stephen, and Walter close behind. Mom drew a bath for me while Mart chose a movie, Stephen and Walter made hot cider, and Daniel walked the dogs again.

We all settled onto the sectional sofa to watch *Dan In Real Life*, one of my favorite movies ever. I loved Steve Carrell, especially when he wasn't primarily funny. Aslan curled up on my lap, and I was asleep before Juliette Binoche even arrived on screen.

BY MORNING, the swelling in my face had gone down, but I looked like I'd come out on the raw end of a boxing match, and I guess, in a way, I had. I was all purple and black around my eye and jawbone, and while it hurt like the dickens, I was secretly a little thrilled because – for reasons I'd never understood – I had always wanted a black eye. I expect it was about the attention.

In fact, I did spend the morning being doted on. Mom and Dad brought me breakfast in bed, and Stephen and Walter had already begun a complete spring cleaning of our house. Mart had arranged to have my favorite comfy chair in the shop – the chair and a half that usually sits by the fiction section and is covered in book-print fabric – to be brought up by the register. Last night, I had felt a bit like royalty. This morning, I was going to feel like someone should be fanning me with palm leaves and feeding me grapes. I kind of liked it.

But my attention for my injury soured late-morning when Miranda came by the shop with the girls. I took one look at her face, largely healed but still showing the faint bruises from her husband's hands and immediately felt terrible for reveling in being hit. The circumstances were different, of course, but I was ashamed of taking the attention I was given when Miranda had needed to be so careful not to draw attention from her husband or anyone who might stir up his anger.

As the twins jogged off to read to each other, their mom and I took a table by the window in the café. I still wasn't up to full force yet, so Marcus was managing things for the most part. Still, I wanted to see how Miranda was doing, and I needed to have a conversation with her about the girls' and our upcoming photo shoot, but also about something more difficult. I wasn't looking forward to this.

And when I dread something, I plow right in, eager to get it over with. I was still calling this little trait "spontaneity." Miranda had barely set our lattes down – drinks she'd insisted on paying for and carrying because of my injury – when I said, "Miranda, I really want to hear all about how you are and what you think of all this news. But first, I need to talk with you about something."

She sat forward and said, "Of course. Are you okay? I'm so sorr—"

"I need to know why you accused Marcus of killing your father." My voice was quiet, almost a whisper. I didn't want to draw attention to us, but I also hated this kind of confrontation, even when I knew I needed to do it.

Miranda looked down at her hands and twisted her fingers. "I don't really know. I mean I've thought about it a lot.

I felt my shoulders drop just a bit. At least she realized something was amiss there. "Yeah?"

"Yeah. I mean I don't think of myself as racist or anything, but when I found out that someone had killed my dad, the first person I thought of was Marcus." She glanced over to the register where he was laughing and ringing up a young boy who looked to buying the entire Brian Jacques *Redwall* series. "I have no idea why."

I took a deep breath. "So you didn't see someone who looked like Marcus running away from Elle's farm stand?"

She shook her head. She let out a shuddering breath. "Even worse. I didn't see anyone running away at all. I wasn't even there."

I tried to keep calm, after all I knew what this woman had lived through. But I was livid. Someone had accused a person I love of something because of—

"Racism," she said. "It was just racist of me to do that."

Her admission set me back on my heels a bit, and I floundered at what to say.

"Yes, it was racist." Marcus had come over to the table, a copy of *Publisher's Weekly* in his hand. "I'm glad you realize that." There was no anger in his voice, no venom. He just sounded tired.

Miranda looked up at him, and then she stood. "I'm sorry. I can't even explain my behavior, much less justify it. I'm very sorry." She put out her hand.

He didn't even wait before shaking her hand, which is more than I was inclined to do at the moment. I kind of still wanted to give her a good talking to. He gave Miranda a small smile and then looked at me. "Someone is asking when we'll have the new Miranda," he looked at the woman across the table, "the new Miranda James mystery."

"We'll order it today. Should come on release day then," I said with a small smile.

"Thanks." He walked away quietly.

"Do you think he'll ever forgive me?" Miranda's voice was very quiet.

"Probably. In time. He's that kind of person." I took a deep breath. "Okay, so before you go, I can get you copies of Robin DiAngelo and Tim Wise's books. They might help you explore why you accused Marcus. They helped me."

She nodded. "I'd like that."

"Plus, well, you need to update your reading list a bit. Girl, that big ole compendium of books you gave me was all ancient stuff. Haven't you read anything new?"

Miranda blushed. "I wasn't allowed to go to the library or anything. No unmonitored internet access allowed, and he kept a tight rein on my spending, so I couldn't buy books either. All I had to read were the books I brought with me when I married Rafe. Couldn't even go to the library because of the computers."

I sighed. "And those were books from your childhood, maybe your mom's books?

"Grandmother's actually. I read a lot when I was a kid, but we got most of our books from the library to save money." She gave me a small smile then. "Still, there are a lot of good books on that list."

I grinned. "I expect so. I'll definitely be getting some of them in. Thanks again for that. But still, we need to get you up to date."

"Most definitely," she said. "I really want to read that one about the girl on the bus."

I laughed and then winced. *"Girl on a Train.* I'll add that to your stack today."

"Great."

"Now, tell me what your plans are." I smiled at my new friend.

We talked for a good bit longer about the ranch and their plans. She and the girls had decided to sell, to move up to Boston with her aunt and start over. "Too many memories here, and I just can't handle the memories of Homer."

I understood. A childhood friend turned killer . . . but also rescuer in a way. That was a lot to live with day-to-day.

We made plans for the girls to come on Tuesday for their photo shoot in the children's section, and then she bought the books I recommended – I added Michelle Alexander's *The New Jim Crow* to the mix, too. As she left, she turned to me and said, "Harvey, really. Thank you. For this," she held up the books and then gestured toward my cheek. "For that, too. I don't know what would have happened when I had to refuse Homer again. The sheriff said he was so convinced he'd done the right thing and that now I'd have to love him." She sighed. "Funny thing was, I've always loved him. Just not like that."

I watched her, Maisy , and Daisy– earrings in again today – walk down the street and wished them well. Marcus came up next to me, bumped my shoulder gently, and handed me the *Publisher's Weekly*. "She's going to be really mad if she doesn't get her new mystery on time."

I looked down at the magazine. "Got it. Let's get the order in."

IT TOOK ME A FEW DAYS, but the pain in my head faded as did my bruises. The blow to my ego for my stupidity took longer to ease, but fortunately, no one thought it necessary to rub it in.

The bookstore kept humming along, and as we moved more fully into the "season" with more tourists coming down to get on the water, sales picked up. We started getting lots of special orders, especially for books about local history, and I started pondering an event for May, a local history gathering, and was thrilled when Lucas agreed to co-coordinate with the Museum as the co-sponsor.

Mom and Dad opted to buy a condo right on the water – close enough for a long walk when we wanted to get together, but not so close that we'd be tempted to pop in on each other just because we didn't feel like cooking. Meanwhile, Stephen and Walter moved into that gorgeous house, and we had frequent cookouts on their deck overlooking that gorgeous view, and I enjoyed many a Mai Tai on a spring evening.

. . .

ONE AFTERNOON, I left the shop about four, as I had started doing after Marcus got his feet fully under him as assistant manager, and began the walk home. I loved that the days were getting longer and that I could look forward to a few hours of reading on the back porch before the sun set. I'd just gotten in Jon Cohen's novel *Harry's Trees*, and I was eager to make up for all the lost reading time I've given to opening the shop.

I had just turned onto my block when a flash of silver caught my eye. I turned and saw the silver C-10 that had stalked me – Homer's truck – cruising down the road in my direction. Without thinking, I began to run. Mayhem, sensing my fear, took off and pulled me toward home. We reached the house just as the truck pulled in my driveway. I fumbled with my keys and had just gotten the door unlocked when a voice said, "Harvey, it's me."

I stopped. Took a deep breath. Turned around and screamed, "Daniel Galena, if you ever scare me like that again . . ."

He was standing a few feet away, stock still with a look of shock on his face. "Was I the reason you took off running? I thought you just wanted to get a little jog in."

"Daniel, when have you ever seen me run for the sake of running?"

He stepped closer. "I'm so sorry, Harvey. I didn't think."

"Why are you in his truck?" I spat. My heart was still pounding, and I didn't have the wherewithal to pull myself together just yet.

"I bought it. For you."

I looked at him. It was my turn to be stunned, and I had so many options for shock. "You bought me a truck? The truck of the man who tried to kill me?" I looked from Daniel to the truck and back again, my anger subsiding into something that felt much more pleasant. "You bought me a truck?"

He smiled. "I did. It was at the police impound and was just released, so I got a great deal. I know you love these old pick-ups, and you're always talking about redeeming the hard things. I thought this was a win-win." He studied my face. "But maybe I was wrong? I can sell it if you don't want it."

I walked toward him, rested my hand on his arm, and then walked over to the truck. "Can we paint it? I've always wanted my truck to be aqua and glossy."

Daniel walked up and slipped his arm around my waist. "We can paint it whatever color you like."

I leaned up, kissed Daniel's cheek, and then climbed in the driver's side door. "Consider this truck redeemed."

BOUND TO EXECUTE

I have this not-yet-explored fascination with garden magazines. Every time I see one and have the cash on hand, I pick it up. I'm such a sucker for those images of great planters and perfect levels of colorful flowers that I have to limit myself to cash-only purchases lest I spend my mortgage money on magazines that I don't have any time to read.

So why I thought I'd start not one but two gardens while also running my own bookstore, I don't know. But I did . . . and I was loving it. At home, my roommate and best friend, Mart, and I had built some raised beds from fence boards that were left behind when we bought the house, and at the shop, I gathered a variety of planters from yard sales and auctions – with the help of my friends Stephen and Walter, denizens of good bargains and great taste – to arrange in front of the bookstore.

At home, the planting was easy. We put in vegetable starts from our friend Elle Heron's farm stand – tomatoes and peppers and one eggplant because I had this vision of suddenly liking the vegetable if I grew it. Plus, we seeded some carrots, beans, and melons, and I got very excited by the prospect of harvesting and then cooking with the food fresh from the yard. I was very optimistic.

The bookstore plants proved more daunting because I wanted to recreate, so very badly, those gorgeous photos from the books. Elle cautioned me, though, about the various light and water needs of the eighty-eight flowers or so that I had dog-eared in the gardening magazines and suggested I go simple. Thus, I stuck with calibrachoa in a beautiful butter yellow and magenta coleus to complement it. I loved the look of those colors, even though – as several enthusiastic (and several other slightly angry) customers pointed out – I had inadvertently given tribute to the Redskins football team. Ravens' fans were angry that I hadn't, apparently, genetically altered flowers to make them teal and black, but I didn't point out that I was a bookseller, not a horticulturist. I also didn't say that I would never support – with my flowers or my money – the Redskins, given their racist mascot and team name. I wasn't always good at holding my tongue, but in this case, I did. No need to make customers angry, after all.

Still, the pots – alongside the bench my friend Woody had made – gave the converted gas station a welcoming feel. Customers often sat out there with a cup of coffee from Rocky's café and enjoyed the spring weather. The first two weeks of May on the Eastern Shore are picture perfect for sitting and basking in the spring sun. Temperatures in the seventies. A slight breeze off the water. Perfect.

In fact, most days when my assistant manager, Marcus, came in, I took my place on that bench for that very reason. Mayhem, my Black Mouth Cur, had figured out that the sun hit the west side of that bench perfectly in the afternoon, so she never hesitated to bed down in a sunbeam while I turned my face toward the sky and soaked in some Vitamin D.

It was in that face-up position that Henri Johnson found me on that early May afternoon. "Hi Harvey," she said as she dropped onto the bench next to me.

I sat up just a little to turn toward her, but quickly resumed my position when she, too, leaned back, closed her eyes, and sighed. "What brings you by, Henri? Need some more books?"

"Not yet, my dear. Bear brought me the last orders, and I'm still working through them. Just hard to stay inside and read when the weather is this nice."

I patted the copy of *Crime and Punishment* next to me. "That's why I always bring a book."

She laughed. "I see how much reading you're getting done at the moment."

I peeked over at my friend and marveled at the beautiful pink tones under her brown skin. Henri had the best complexion of anyone I knew, by far. I'd asked her once what she used, and she'd held up a pile of wool roving from next to her spinning wheel. "Lanolin. All natural."

Henri was a weaver – a really good one. One of her pieces was the runner for our dining table at home, but just this week, Mart and I had talked about asking her to make us a new piece for the table, something lighter for summer.

We sat quietly for several minutes as the sun warmed us. I relished these days before humidity. I had grown up just north of here, and I knew a Maryland summer was not something to be trifled with, especially if you had curly hair like I did. Humidity and curls are not a good combination. But these perfectly warm days, I could do with months of those.

Eventually, though, I felt the tell-tale tingle of a sunburn coming on and thought it best to put on my ball cap and begin the walk home. As I sat forward, Henri stood, too. "Thanks for that moment of rest, Harvey. I saw you here on my way to the bank and just couldn't resist."

"Well, Henri, I'm honored to have had your company on the bench to bask. Let's do it again before the town becomes a sauna."

"Deal." She gave my arm a pat before she headed on up the street, a blue bank envelope in her hand.

Seeing her deposit envelope made me glance at my watch – 4:45 – just enough time to get an extra deposit in before the weekend. I bustled inside and headed for the register. Marcus was just ringing up a sale, so I gave him a wink as I settled onto the stool behind him to wait.

As always, he had hand-sold the customer some of his favorite books. Right now, he was on a Louise Erdrich kick, and I saw that the woman was leaving with copies of both *The Round House* and her new book, *The Night Watchman*. The woman was smiling, and I knew Marcus had secured another customer for the store. For about the millionth time I thought how lucky I was to have met him and to have been able to convince him to work with me.

He smiled at me. "Whatcha need, Ms. B? Forget something?"

"Nope. Just decided to do an extra deposit before the weekend. Feeling flush with our big sales this week." I laughed. It hadn't exactly been a big enough week that I could afford a yacht like some of those now coming into the St. Marin's marina for the season, but each week, we were selling a bit more, and I hoped by our one-year anniversary in the fall we'd be ready to bring on a third employee.

"Sounds good." He leaned down, unlocked the cabinet door, and then opened the small safe we kept there. "Always good to keep your cash in the bank, Mama says. Less likely to spend it that way."

Marcus's mom, Josie, was a regular columnist in our monthly newsletter. Her book reviews were almost as good as her son's, and I loved her humor and the wisdom it usually hid within.

"Well, if Josie says it's wise, then it must be doubly so." I patted Marcus on his shoulder blade. "You been working out, Marcus? Seems like you might be beefing up a bit."

A flash of color ran up under Marcus's walnut skin. "Maybe a little." His eyes darted over to the café behind me, and I smiled.

"Ah, I see. Well, it looks good on you." Marcus and café owner Rocky had been dating for a few weeks now, and from the pep in their steps and Marcus's newly acquired interest in weight-lifting, it seemed like things were going well.

I slid the cash and checks into our red bank envelope and made a note of what was there before heading to the door. "See you tomorrow." I waved at Marcus and went out below the dinging bell.

Mayhem's sunbeam had moved on, so she was ready to walk. I slid her leash out of the custom-made holder that Woody had added to the bench when he'd realized how much Mayhem loved laying by it and headed in Henri's footsteps to the bank.

It was just a few doors down Main Street to the bank, but it was 4:55 now – and banks didn't make a habit of staying open a minute late, especially not ours. The bank manager, Wilma Painter, was a fastidious, rule-following woman, and none of the business owners in town trifled with her if we could help it. She'd been known to literally slam the bank door on a customer's hand if they dared to try and open it a minute past five.

A woman in her fifties, she had apparently decided to fight the signs of aging with coal-black hair-dye, and unfortunately, Wilma was a woman prone to glistening, as my mother delicately called sweating. So on a warm day, or when things in the bank went a little awry of Wilma's strict standards, rivulets of black stain ran down her cheekbones. I always felt a little bad for her, but I didn't know how – or have the courage – to suggest a visit to a professional salon lest my accounts be closed immediately.

I bustled into the bank lobby at 4:56 and breathed a sigh of relief to see no one ahead of me in line. Some businesses have the, "If you're in the door before closing" policy, but not Wilma's bank. She would march you right out the door at five p.m. if your transaction wasn't finished. I had found that out the hard way one day when she'd grabbed my arm, not gently, and walked me out the door, shutting it snugly after she said, "We reopen on Monday at nine a.m."

The teller gave me a tight smile as I approached. "Hi Cynthia. Sorry to be cutting it so close."

The young woman, who was a frequent visitor to my bookstore's romance section, said, "It's okay. I can count fast," and then proceeded to count my deposit with the lightning speed that the three minutes left in her work day required. She printed the slip just as the clock over her head read 4:59, and I turned to go. But just then, I heard shouting from the direction of Wilma's office.

I turned to see what the commotion was about just as Henri came storming out of the office. Wilma followed behind her, her voice even but steely. "Ms. Johnson, I'll appreciate that you speak to me with respect. This is a place of business."

Henri turned, opened her mouth as if to say something, and then spun back around and walked out of the building.

I stood, dumbfounded, in the middle of the lobby until Wilma spotted me. "Ms. Beckett, please close your mouth and leave. It is 5:02 p.m.," she said as she checked her watch, "and you are now in violation of bank policy. Remain any longer, and I will have to call the police and ask that you be removed."

I lowered my chin and looked at the bank manager from under my eyebrows, but I knew there was no value in giving her a piece of my mind, even if I did relish the idea of Sheriff Mason having to come escort me out for being in the bank at 5:02 p.m. The sheriff and I were good friends, and I knew for a fact that he harbored no deep affection for Wilma Painter. Still, I wasn't in the mood to ruin my Friday night with a stand-off, so I turned, thanked Cynthia again, and went out the door.

Mayhem was waiting by the tree to which I'd tied her, but she was turned back up the street and pulling at her leash. I looked in the direction she was straining and saw Henri leaning up against the wall of the bookstore. Her shoulders were heaving.

I gathered Mayhem and quickly headed that way. "Henri, are you okay? Do you want to come inside and sit down?"

When she lifted her head I saw, though, that she wasn't crying. No, this woman was furious, and she was taking long, hard breaths to, it seemed, calm down. "I'm sorry, Harvey, but that woman."

I nodded. "She is something. Just threatened to have Tuck come and escort me out."

Henri shook her head. "She is really unbelievable." She took a hard breath and dropped her shoulders. "I wouldn't want this getting around town, but she just threatened to foreclose on the co-op."

"What?!" The art co-op down the street was one of the biggest attractions in St. Marin's. Henri had a studio there, and so did our friend Cate, a local photographer known for her portraits. "Why?"

Henri gritted her teeth. "She says that we are behind on our mortgage payments, but that can't be right, can it? I mean, Cate is on top of everything. I can't imagine her missing a payment."

I agreed. Cate had quickly become one of my dearest friends, and she was one of the most organized, thoughtful people I knew. She would never risk putting the co-op or the artists it served at risk. "I can't imagine that either. There must be some other explanation."

Henri met my eye. "You're right. Thanks, Harvey. It's just the way Wilma talked to me, like I was an idiot."

"I know. She is ridiculous." I smiled. "We can figure this all out, though. I'm sure there's some simple story here."

She nodded, then looked at her watch. "Shoot. I'm afraid I can't figure it out now, though. Bear has one of those fancy hospital dinners, and I have to get home and get ready."

I clasped her arm, and we walked up Main Street to the co-op. "Don't worry. Cate and Lucas are coming to my place for dinner tonight. If it's okay with you, I'll tell her what happened and see what she says. Email you later with the story?"

Henri squeezed my hand on her arm. "Oh, that would be great, Harvey. Thanks." She turned to me. "And thanks for calming me down." She gave me a quick hug and then scratched Mayhem behind the ears. "Talk to you tomorrow."

"Definitely. And I'll email tonight for sure."

She hurried down the sidewalk and got into her old, green Jaguar. I waved as she pulled by and then took a deep breath. At least we'd have something to talk about at dinner.

I pulled my phone out of my back pocket. I still had a little time before I needed to go home, so I pointed my feet toward the mechanic's shop at the end of the street. That was all the signal

Mayhem needed to head toward her best friend, Taco, the Bassett Hound. I didn't blame her though. A certain handsome mechanic kind of made me want to run, too.

Daniel was under the front of a blue sedan when we arrived. I could just see his denim-clad legs sticking out. Next to him, the prostrate body of the Bassett Hound lay as if waiting to hand him the next tool . . . well, except for the floppy ear over his eye. Taco was not much good at assisting with anything except weighing down objects and nap training. Still, he was excellent company.

Mayhem wasted no time and stretched out beside him. "I brought another useless assistant for you."

"Oh, hi," Daniel said as he began to slide out on his roller-thingy. I knew that slider contraption he used to get under cars had a name, and I'd even asked, twice. But I'd forgotten both times since I had no compartments for car-related info in my brain, well, unless it related to a book. When I'd read *The Myth of Solid Ground* by David Ulin – an amazing book about earthquakes – I'd learned that James Dean died in a Porsche Spyder on the San Andreas fault, and I had never forgotten. Give me a story, and I'll remember. Otherwise, I couldn't tell an alternator from a brake caliper.

Daniel stood and eyed the two dogs beside him. "Useless, those two. Completely useless."

I stepped forward and gave him a kiss on the cheek, taking a second to breath in that scent of oil and aftershave that I'd come to love even before I'd been willing to tell the man wearing them that I felt the same about him. That hurdle in our relationship had been crossed a few weeks back, though, and now we were sliding into that phase that was about resting easy in affection but not pushing too hard for the next step. I liked this stage, secure and steady with not much pressure.

"Utterly," I said as he leaned over and kissed my cheek.

"To what do I owe the pleasure of this visit?" Daniel asked as he wiped his hands on a blue rag. The man collected rags like they were gold, and I was grateful since I'd been able to gift him all the frayed and stained hand towels at our house without guilt.

"We were just out and about with a little time to kill." I tried to sound nonchalant.

"Oh yeah. Since when do you have time to kill? I mean I appreciate the visit, but wouldn't you rather be squeezing in a chapter of your latest read before dinner?"

He had a point. Ever since the shop had gotten its feet under it and Marcus had begun working full-time, I'd delved back into my reading life with gusto. Daniel, not much of a reader himself, couldn't figure out why I had this obsession with books, but I couldn't figure out his obsession with cars, so I wagered we were even. "Well, yeah, okay. This weird thing happened with Henri at the bank."

I told him about Henri's fight with Wilma and the missing payments. "Doesn't seem like Cate to let something like that slip," he said as he heaved Taco to a standing position before starting to turn off the shop lights.

"That's what I said. She's just too organized for that."

He slipped an only slightly dirty arm around my waist as I encouraged Mayhem to standing with her leash. "You're going to ask her tonight, right?"

"Yep. Sure am. And speaking of which, I better get home and get the hamburgers formed up. I'm adding steak sauce and tucking cheese in the middle. I feel so fancy."

He grinned. "Need a hand? I mean, I'd like to shower, but I can come on if that would help."

I smiled. "You go shower. I can handle the burgers, and I have an audiobook to listen to while I cook."

"Of course you do," he said, giving me a quick kiss before I went out the door. "See you at six-thirty."

He gave a wave as he bent down to lift Taco, who had returned to his previous prone position in the ten seconds that Daniel and I were talking.

MAYHEM PULLED me home with her incessant sniffing, which apparently wore her out because when we got the house, she went right to her dog bed and collapsed. Aslan, my cat, was less than thrilled to be displaced from her makeshift bed in the sun, but the dog was not to be dissuaded. Aslan begrudgingly took up her place on the cashmere throw on my reading chair. Oh, to have the life of one of my pets.

I opened up the e-lending app for the St. Marin's library and click on Patrick Ness's *The Rest of Us Just Live Here.* I'd long been an audiobook listener, but it had taken me a while to warm to checking out audiobooks electronically from the library. I don't really know why I'd stalled – this was the best thing, even if the selection was a bit limited. I knew libraries thrived on circulation numbers, so checking out my audiobooks when I could made sense. Plus, the due date made me listen more and, thus, read more books. It was a win-win.

I had just flipped the burgers in the skillet when I heard car doors slam and the skitter of Mayhem's nails as she went to welcome everyone. In came most of the people I loved: Mart; Stephen and Walter; Cate and her husband, Lucas; my parents, Sharon and Burt; and, of course, Daniel. I glanced at the clock on the microwave – six-thirty on the dot. A punctual bunch, these.

Mart brought in four bottles of wine from the winery where

she worked, including a chardonnay that I loved. Mom and Dad brought salad as requested. Stephen and Walter came bearing some steamed green beans with dill and lemon, and Lucas and Cate carried in two bakery boxes that were, without a doubt, the best cupcakes in all the world. Lucas was the director at the maritime museum in town, but I was not the only person who said he could open a cupcake shop in a heartbeat.

The dogs – Mayhem and Taco – and their two buddies, Sidecar, Mom and Dad's rescue, and Sasquatch, Cate and Lucas's Minia-ture Schnauzer, went right to the water bowl before draping themselves over the cluster of dog beds in the corner of the living room. They were sleeping soundly before we even got the plates out.

This had become our new Friday night ritual, and even in just a month's worth of Friday evenings, we'd fallen into a routine. Stephen and Walter set the table while Mart and Dad got drinks. Mom helped me plate up the burgers and fixings, and Daniel fed the pups under the careful and skeptical eye of Aslan, who could not be bribed – even with tuna – to eat until she had her kitchen back to herself.

We weren't a formal crowd, so everyone grabbed mismatched plates and filled them up before taking seats on the couch and floor in the living room. We didn't have enough dining room chairs for everyone, and also, it felt cozier, more fun, to just picnic in the living room.

I forced myself to wait to ask Cate about the co-op until the second bottle of wine was open, but then my curiosity – a trait my mother had always called nosiness – got the better of me. "Cate, I ran into Henri today. She got into a real hullaballoo with Wilma over at the bank."

"She did? That doesn't seem like Henri." She took a sip of wine.

"But then again, it does seem like Wilma, so . . . what was the ruckus about?"

It was my turn to take a sip of wine. "Well, I told Henri I'd ask you about it and let her know, but apparently, Wilma said the bank is going to foreclose on the co-op because the mortgage hasn't been paid."

I put my wine glass up to my mouth and tilted it back both as shield and salve.

"What in the—?" Cate was on her feet faster than I could blink.

Lucas stood with her and put a hand on her arm. "This must be a mistake, Cate. We can clear it up first thing Monday. Or we can call Wilma at home, if we can find her number."

Cate slapped his hand away. "Of course it's a mistake. And any self-respecting banker who had been dealing with another business for as long as they have should know that there's a mistake. How dare she threaten to foreclose without talking to me! How dare she give that information to anyone but me!" Cate's voice had gotten very quiet, and I could see from the set of her jaw that the quiet belied the rage.

I let out a long breath, hoping that might inspire Cate to do the same, but instead, she locked eyes on me. "You say Wilma Painter had the gall to bring this up just before the close of business on a Friday? That woman is unbelievable. Unbelievable and cowardly. When I get my hands on her—"

"We all know this is a mistake, Cate." Daniel's voice was firm and even. "And we all have your back. We won't let Wilma do anything to the co-op." He wasn't a man of many words, but when he spoke, people listened. The energy in the room was quelled to only slightly uncomfortable.

Cate's eyes welled up. "I know. Thank you, Daniel, but it's a bank. Banks are ruthless institutions. If they think I haven't been paying our mortgage . . ." Her eyes snapped up to mine. "Oh, Harvey. How was Henri? She must have been horrified."

"Apoplectic might be a better adjective. She knew there was an error, and she was furious that Wilma would contend that it was some lack of judgment or moral diligence that caused this situation." I waited a minute and hoped there was enough oxygen in the room to handle my next question. "I told her I'd ask you about it and let her know. Do you have any idea what happened?"

My question brought Cate to her knee on the floor. Lucas handed back her wine glass, and she took a long sip. "I don't. I send the payment with the deposit on the last day of the month. Always have."

Stephen leaned forward. "You don't pay it electronically?"

Cate shook her head. "Nope. I knew I could have, and Wilma put some pressure on me to do that – I expect I'll hear a big ole hair-dye-stained 'I told you' so on that one now – but it always seemed easier to just write up the transfer form and put it in with the cash. That way, there was a paper trail."

I stared down into my now-empty wine glass. "Did you take the deposits yourself?"

Cate's eyes whipped up to mine. "No. No, I didn't." I could see the rage building behind her eyes again. "I had Ollie do it because I like to work on my images in the afternoon. I'm so stupid."

"Ollie – the kid with the gauges in his ears?" Lucas asked, trying to sound neutral. But from the look on his face, I could tell he was thinking what we were thinking, *Why would you trust that knucklehead with anything, much less bank deposits?* I'd talked with him several times, and while he was nice enough, he always seemed a little distracted.

Cate sighed. "Yep, he's the one. We never have much cash to deposit. A couple hundred dollars a day since our artists get paid directly. Mostly, it's just sales from the few gift items and rent from the artisans. I checked the account the first few times he went, and everything was good. Then, I kind of assumed we were fine. Apparently, we were not."

Walter adjusted his hips on the couch next to me. "So he just didn't turn in the transfer request for the mortgage payments and then withdrew the money that should have gone to the mortgage." He ran his fingers through his hair. "For a kind of dumb kid, that's a pretty smart move. You wouldn't even notice because the amount would have been the same in the account, unless you checked your mortgage statement, I mean."

I banged my wine glass onto the table. "But wouldn't the bank have warned you that you missed a payment? Or several? I mean they don't want to foreclose, right? It's not good money for them. So much better to get your mortgage payment and all that interest." I looked to Stephen for affirmation.

"Right. Foreclosure isn't profitable for the bank. It just staunches the hemorrhage of money from someone who doesn't pay. They definitely would have sent notices."

Daniel's voice was very tiny when he spoke. "I expect that Wilma had those sent by hand with Ollie."

"What?!" Cate was on her feet again, and I was glad when Lucas took her wine glass away. She had looked ready to throw it.

"That's what she did when I missed a payment for the shop." He looked at me quickly. "I had the flu and didn't get my transfer done in time. When I went in the next week to set things right, the teller handed me a late payment notice. No email. No call. Just a piece of paper."

"Probably too cheap to pay for the stamp, the old bat. So she

probably gave the man who was stealing from you the notifica-
tions that would have let you know he was stealing. Unbelievable," Mart shouted.

Now I felt like throwing my wine glass.

"I think that's probably illegal," Walter said quietly. "A breach of
confidentiality at least. That may be your best way forward here,
Cate. A lawyer arguing that the bank failed in its due diligence."
Walter had sold a very successful construction business in San
Francisco when he and Stephen had recently moved to St.
Marin's, so I expected he knew what he was talking about.

Mom and Dad had sat quietly through this whole exchange, but
now Dad's voice was clear. "I've just texted Sheriff Mason. He's
on his way over."

It took me a minute to figure out why Dad had asked the sheriff
to come when this was clearly a business issue. Then I realized
what he was saying. "Ollie is a thief," I whispered.

"Maybe. Maybe not," Dad said. "But it's time to hand this query
over the authorities, don't you think?"

Daniel, Mart, Stephen, and Walter looked at me pointedly. I had
a habit of doing a bit of investigating on my own, and my
friends did not like it.

"Good idea, Dad." I stood and walked over to Cate. "We'll figure
this out, Cate. The co-op is going to be fine."

She leaned her head on my shoulder, and I hoped I was right.

**Order Bound To Execute, Book 3 in the St. Marin's Cozy
Mystery Series here - books2read.com/boundtoexecute**

HARVEY AND MARCUS'S BOOK
RECOMMENDATIONS

*H*ere, you will find all the books and authors recommended in *Entitled To Kill* to add to your never-ending to-read-list!

- *The Water Dancer* by Ta-Nehisi Coates
- *Save Me The Plums* by Ruth Reichl
- *Eat This Poem* by Nicole Gulotta
- *Marley and Me* by John Grogan
- *The Art of Racing in the Rain* by Garth Stein
- *Dinosaurs Before Dark* Magic Tree House 1 by Mary Pope Osborne
- *The Secret Garden* by Frances Hodgson Burnett
- *Home Front* by Kristin Hannah
- *Cloister Walk* by Kathleen Norris
- *An American Marriage* by Tayari Jones
- *Senlin Ascends* by Josiah Bancroft
- The His Dark Materials Trilogy by Philip Pullman
- *Slaves in the Family* by Edward Ball
- *Murder by the Book* by Lauren Elliott
- *Mrs. Rumphius* by Barbara Cooney
- *Out of the Silent Planet* by C.S. Lewis

- *To Kill A Mockingbird* by Harper Lee
- *In Cold Blood* by Truman Capote
- *Hiawatha and the Peacemaker* by Robbie Robertson
- *City Of Ghosts* by Victoria Schwab
- *Stamped from the Beginning* by Ibram X. Kendi
- *Trail of Lightning* by Rebecca Roanhorse
- *American Pastoral* by Philip Roth
- *A Man Called Ove* by Fredrik Backman
- *The Boys of my Youth* by JoAnn Beard
- *Piggies* by Audrey Wood
- *Say You're One Of Them* by Uwem Akpan
- *Redwall* by Brian Jacques
- *Murder Past Due* by Miranda James
- *White Like Me* by Tim Wise
- *The New Jim Crow* by Michelle Alexander
- *White Fragility* by Robin DiAngelo
- *Amazing Grace* by Kathleen Norris
- *Girl on a Train* by Paula Hawkins

I have personally read each of these titles and recommend them highly. Feel free to drop me a line at acfbookens@andilit.com and let me know if you read any or have books you think I should read. Thanks!

Happy Reading,

ACF

WANT TO READ ABOUT HARVEY'S FIRST SLEUTHING EXPEDITION?

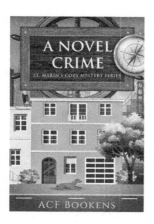

Join my Cozy Up email group for weekly book recs & a FREE copy of *A Novel Crime*, the prequel to the St. Marin's Cozy Mystery Series.

Sign-up here - https://bookens.andilit.com/CozyUp

ALSO BY ACF BOOKENS

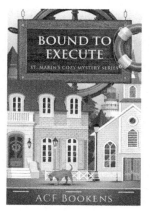

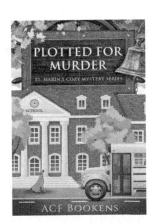

ABOUT THE AUTHOR

ACF Bookens lives in the Blue Ridge Mountains of Virginia, where the mountain tops remind her that life is a rugged beauty of a beast worthy of our attention. When she's not writing, she enjoys watching her husband and son ride the tractor, cross-stitching while she binge-watches police procedurals, and reading everything she can get her hands on. Find her at bookens.andilit.com.

facebook.com/BookensCozyMysteries

Made in the USA
Columbia, SC
30 June 2020